Piers had fall...
still pulled do...

Brute, Alyssia tho... ...en she
picked up the tall g... ...d sedately to
the water's edge, fille... with ice-cold water
and returned. She carefully tilted his cap
back, held the glass about one foot over him
and poured.

He spluttered back into life, sitting up
abruptly.

'There,' she said sweetly, relishing every word
of her parting shot. 'We wouldn't want you to
get sunburnt, now, would we?'

WE HOPE you're enjoying our new addition to our Contemporary Romance series—stories which take a light-hearted look at the Zodiac and show that love can be written in the stars!

Every month you can get to know a different combination of star-crossed lovers, with one story that follows the fortunes of a hero or a heroine when they embark on the romance of a lifetime with somebody born under another sign of the Zodiac. This month features a sizzling love-affair between **VIRGO** and **ARIES**.

To find out more fascinating facts about this month's featured star sign, turn to the back pages of this book. . .

ABOUT THIS MONTH'S AUTHOR

Cathy Williams was born in November, under the sign of Scorpio. Scorpions are known for their passionate temperament, their love of life, and, of course, the sting in their tail!

She has been married for many years to her husband, Richard, who, as a Libran, counterbalances her fiery temperament with his more even-tempered one. Cathy was born in the Caribbean and has never lost her love for the *joie de vivre* and vitality of its people. It is the setting for many of her romance stories.

Cathy and Richard have one child, a daughter, Charlotte.

A FRENCH ENCOUNTER

BY

CATHY WILLIAMS

MILLS & BOON LIMITED
ETON HOUSE   18–24 PARADISE ROAD
RICHMOND   SURREY   TW9 1SR

First published in Great Britain 1992
by Mills & Boon Limited

© Cathy Williams 1992

Australian copyright 1992
Philippine copyright 1992
This edition 1992

ISBN 0 263 77656 5

Set in 10 on 11½ pt Linotron Times
01-9208-52896 Z

Typeset in Great Britain by Centracet, Cambridge
Made and printed in Great Britain

CHAPTER ONE

ALYSSIA dropped her expensive Gucci bags at her feet, wiped the beads of perspiration from her brow, and thought, Damn!

The flight from London to the Nice-Côte d'Azur airport in the south of France had been long-winded and tiring, with delays at either end. The taxi ride from the airport to the little village where she was staying, only six kilometres from Nice, had been uncomfortable because the air-conditioning in the car had broken down three days before her arrival and was waiting to be repaired, and all in all her last vestiges of good humour had finally bitten the dust as she'd stood in front of the house and realised that it hadn't finished being built.

It was interestingly designed, true enough, a charming affair of pink stucco backing against the hill, and with its own private path snaking towards the sea, but there was still something unfinished about it.

She wrinkled her nose in irritation, wishing that her father had had the foresight to warn her that it had not been fully completed, instead of waving her on her way with a cheery remark about how the change would do her good.

She was hot and sticky and tired, and the thought of change in the form of no running water was not appealing. How would she cope?

She had lived her twenty-two years surrounded by life's little luxuries, all the wonderful comforts that money could buy, and she didn't see herself as the sort of healthy, hardy girl who could endure too many minor inconveniences with a cheery smile.

Still, she thought, what else was she going to do? She was fed up with her life in London, a whirlwind of social engagements which recently had seemed unbearably shallow, and more to the point she needed time to put her engagement to Jonathan, or rather her decision to break it off, into perspective.

Her father had been right; she needed the change.

She picked up the bags at her feet and plodded to the white wooden door, feeling in her bag for the key.

The first thing she would do, she decided, was take a walk into the little village and stock up on some foodstuffs. Things always looked better on a full stomach, and right now she was ravenous.

She slipped the key into the lock and was about to turn it when she looked down and realised with surprise that the door was open. Very slightly.

Damn, damn, damn, more proof that the place was being worked on. She was fed up, she was hungry, and now she would have to confront a horde of troublesome workmen lounging about the house, banging nails, screwing screws and making ribald comments when what she had thought she was escaping to was a slice of peace and solitude.

She felt the fire inside her begin to burn again and she pushed the door wide open, her mouth ready to frame a few well-chosen words on the importance of finishing jobs on time. To hell with her resolution not to let her temper get the better of her.

She tried to count to ten, and tried even harder to remember what that astrologer had said to her, but had that astrologer really known what she was talking about anyway? It had seemed a good idea at the time, a bit of expensive and unusual fun with some of her friends, and sure, she had been intrigued when she had been told that she should beware of her fiery nature's setting alight a situation which would become frighteningly uncontrollable, but that was three days ago.

Right now it would have taken more than a memory of someone else's predictions to have any effect on the blazing anger stirring in her at the prospect of sweaty workmen and a ruined holiday.

She took a deep breath, and pushed open the door, quite prepared to leave the horde of lounging workmen in no doubt that they had ruined her holiday, but she didn't have the opportunity to utter a word, because the man standing in front of her said briefly, 'I've been expecting you, Miss Stanley.'

The coolly spoken words were like a bucket of ice-cold water thrown in her face, but instead of restoring her composure it had the opposite effect of stoking her anger all the more.

She stood stock-still and pursed her lips, her eyes taking in the powerful build of this stranger, tall and athletic-looking, with his faded T-shirt exposing strong, tanned arms. Now who the hell was this guy?

He had none of the prettiness of the boys she was accustomed to seeing in her circle of friends. Just the opposite; there was something aggressively hard and very rugged about his face. As though he was a man who lived life to the full, and basically didn't care overmuch for what anyone else thought about him.

The grey eyes were looking back at her, assessing her, she realised angrily, with equal frankness.

Just who did he think he was? No one looked at her like that! There was just enough boldness in his stare to border on the arrogant, and she clenched her fists at her sides.

'And who,' she asked coldly, 'might you be? *You*

may have been expecting me, but I sure as hell wasn't expecting you!'

She folded her arms across her breasts and didn't go one step further. The man looked dangerous, and with just the two of them in this house, with no one around within screaming distance, she wasn't taking any chances.

The ice in her voice had no effect on him whatsoever. Normally that particular tone could quell a charging bull at ten paces, but this man, she thought, must have skin as thick as leather because he didn't look in the least bit intimidated.

In fact, she noticed, there was something ever so slightly contemptuous about his expression.

The mere idea sent another arrow of anger shooting through her. She was positively trembling with rage, and she could feel her nails piercing into the flesh of her arm.

'Well,' she snapped, 'are you going to tell me who you are, or do I have to call the constable?'

'You'd need a very loud voice,' the man said, unperturbed, 'because the phone hasn't been installed yet.' The contempt was less concealed now, and Alyssia looked at him with loathing.

'What are you doing here?' she asked with as much control as she could muster.

This time he did the unthinkable. He turned his back to her and walked off into the open-plan living-room, with its huge glass patio doors that led on to the front garden.

'*Excuse me.*' she yelled, hurrying behind the departing back, 'where do you think you're going?' He was walking purposefully through into the garden, a huge lawn with an abundance of mimosa and roses, and untamed greenery bordering the edges.

In the distance Alyssia could see the flat blue sea, and at the far side the path leading down to the cove.

She stopped in her tracks, absolutely refusing to go one step further, and waited for him to turn around. Her images of that horde of ribald workmen looked positively endearing next to this man.

He did, though there was nothing deferential in his action. Whoever he was, and he had still not seen fit to explain that little detail, he was making no effort to afford her the awestruck courtesy to which she was accustomed. In fact, there was more than a hint of insolence lurking in the grey depths of his eyes when he spoke.

'Dear, oh, dear,' he drawled with mocking disdain, 'what am I thinking? You're hot, tired, hungry very probably, and here I am, not answering any of your well-founded questions. Very rude of me.'

'Yes!' she agreed in a high voice. 'Very.'

'And, of course, I can tell that you're not at all accustomed to having any of your questions ignored, are you?'

Alyssia opened her mouth to give him a piece of her mind at this further show of arrogance—in fact, to give him the sack, because his mere presence here implied that he was working for her father, and so, in an indirect manner, for herself—but he didn't allow her the chance.

'Sit down, before you buckle under the weight of that ego of yours, and I'll explain everything.'

He pointed to a wooden bench perched at the edge of the grassy slope that led to the cove.

'How dare you?' she spluttered, finding herself following him nevertheless.

She had completely forgotten how tired and hungry she was. All her energies were too busy focusing on how much she disliked this man, who had not even deigned to tell her his name as yet, even though he knew hers.

Even so, as she followed the straight line of his back, seeing the way he moved smoothly and economically, the black hair carelessly swept back and curling at the nape of his neck, she felt a brief *frisson* of something she could not explain.

He waited for her to sit down, and then remained standing, one foot on the bench.

'I don't know who you think you are,' she began, deciding to take the initiative, 'but I can tell you that my father won't be at all pleased with your attitude. You're rude, you're insulting, and quite frankly I won't tolerate it.'

He raised one eyebrow expressively, as though to say, 'Oh, really?' and Alyssia could quite easily have hit him.

But there was something vaguely forbidding about him. She couldn't be at all sure that giving in to such an impulse would have the desired effect. In fact, she had a disturbing idea that he might very well hit her back.

She shielded her eyes and stared up at him, and felt that peculiar shiver of awareness again.

What on earth was wrong with her? She hoped she wasn't coming down with something, because that would be the last straw.

'There are still some things to be done in the house,' he said calmly, 'a few cupboards left to build, some wiring, and I've stayed behind to finish it all.'

'Why didn't my father tell me that you were going to be here?' she asked petulantly, thinking that at least he would only be around during the daytime, and she could avoid him completely without too much trouble.

He shrugged and looked at her with those unfathomable grey eyes. What was he thinking? Whatever it was, it wasn't what she expected from a man.

When men looked at her it was normally with admiration; when they spoke to her it was with the awe they felt when confronted by her beauty. Because she *was* beautiful, with her flaxen blonde hair tumbling down her back and those unusual dark eyes and eyebrows that gave her a look of the exotic. She knew it, and had become quite accustomed to the adulation it inspired.

But there was nothing in the least admiring in this man's assessment of her.

'I don't even know your name,' she said tightly.

'Morrison.' He stood up straight and thrust his hands into the pockets of his faded jeans. 'Piers Morrison.'

'And, Mr Morrison, exactly how long do you think these finishing touches are going to take? Because I came here to get away from people, not to bump into them.'

'Why do you want to get away from people?' he asked, staring at her.

'That,' Alyssia replied coldly, 'is hardly the business of the carpenter working in my house, is it?'

This time he grinned at her, a slow smile that made the breath catch in her throat, because it transformed the unyielding contours of his face into devilish charm. She hurriedly diverted her eyes towards the sea to hide her sudden confusion.

'I've never been called a carpenter before,' he mused, 'but I suppose there's something in the description. As for how much longer I'll be here, who knows? However long it takes me to finish my job.'

'What kind of answer is that?'

'The kind of answer you're going to get.' He smiled

coolly, and it was a smile that somehow managed to convey a ruthless hardness in him that wasn't used to compromise and wasn't going to start now.

'Fine,' she snapped. The glare from the sun was beginning to give her a headache, and she wished that she had never undertaken this ridiculous trip.

Why had she, anyway? Most girls would have envied her lifestyle. She was beautiful, wealthy and popular. If she had had any sense she would still be in London, planning her next social function with her friends, instead of slinking off to the south of France because she had felt claustrophobic, because she needed to formulate a way of telling her fiancé that their engagement was off. Those were things that had not necessitated a vacation in the south of France.

'Just make sure,' she continued imperiously, 'that you only work until five o'clock, so that at least I can have some privacy in the evenings.'

'Oh,' he said, one dark eyebrow raised, 'didn't your father tell you anything at all? No, I suppose not. But I happen to be living here.'

'You're what?'

'I don't intend to repeat myself. You heard well enough the first time.'

'You can't,' Alyssia said flatly, slapping down the impulse to become hysterical.

Why hadn't that damned astrologer warned her about this? Any astrologer worth her salt would have predicted this man's presence and told her to steer clear.

'Sorry, my girl, I am, and you'll just have to get used to the idea. Now, are you finished with your questions?'

Finished with her questions? She hadn't started! And she wasn't 'his girl'. More show of his contempt for her! She didn't have to stand for it!

'My father will pay for you to have a room in the village.'

'No can do. I work until late into the night most nights. You'll just have to put up with my company, or else. . .'

'Or else what?' she flared.

'Or else return to London where your little queen-bee act would be more appreciated.'

'You. . .you. . .!' She stood up and raised her hand, but before she could slap him roundly on his face she felt her wrist caught in a vice-like grip.

'Let's get a few things straight,' he said in a grim voice; 'we'll be sharing this house, whether you like it or not, and I don't intend to be the subject of your childish ill-temper. That sort of thing might work with your little clique of boyfriends, but it won't work with me. If you can't be civil, then keep out of my way.'

Alyssia felt the blood rush to her hairline. No one, but no one, had ever spoken to her like that before, and she didn't like it, all the more because she knew he had a point. Her reactions had been childish, the behaviour of a spoiled brat, but he had a cheek to point it out when he was only an employee of her father's. And, by extension, of hers.

Still, his words stung.

'That could cost you your job,' she threw at him.

He released her abruptly, as though the physical contact was distasteful, and said in the same flat, grim voice, 'Reporting back to Daddy? Have you never been criticised in your life before?'

'No,' she blurted out, instantly regretting her response. This man didn't deserve it.

'I'd feel sorry for you, but I'm afraid I don't have much time for the poor little rich girl syndrome. As for reporting to Daddy, you go right ahead, though you might find that what he has to say isn't much to your liking.' He looked as though he was going to say more, but he didn't. He walked back into the house.

Alyssia spun around. This man was more than unbearable. He was impertinent, rude and arrogant.

For some reason, though, she found herself following him, once again, even though she would have been far better staying where she was and letting the anger drain out of her.

'I had no idea that philosophy was also part of a carpenter's trade.'

She had tied her hair back with a pale blue ribbon, to match the cool, summery blue dress, and she pulled it off, shaking her long hair free.

Piers turned around to face her, and for a split second his glance swept over her with appreciation, but the moment was gone so quickly that she thought she must have imagined it.

'I don't need to be Plato to see the obvious,' he said coldly. 'You've had everything and everyone your way from much too young, and it hasn't prepared you for the big, wide world. But you can't spend your life only mixing with people who flatter your ego. Sooner or later you're going to find out that life just doesn't work that way.'

'Well, thank you so much for that valuable insight,' she said sarcastically. 'Any more profound truths to impart before I go upstairs and have a bath?'

The mocking little smile was back on his face, and his eyes had resumed their watchful, vaguely arrogant look.

'Only that I'll be eating lunch in about an hour's time,' he said. 'You're quite welcome to share it with me, provided your manners have improved by then.'

Alyssia ignored the insult. 'A chef as well,' she said

sweetly, looking up at him and thinking that he must be awfully tall because she was five-ten, and he towered above her.

'I'm a man of many talents.'

Their eyes locked together for an instant, and Alyssia felt suddenly dizzy, as though the breath had been knocked out of her, then she regained her self-control, and replied politely, 'I'll be down for lunch.'

She walked past him into the tiny hallway and picked up her bags, noticing with relief that he wasn't around when she fled up the narrow wooden stairs to one of the three bedrooms, the one furthest away from his.

She shut the door behind her, and, in the solitude of the bedroom, felt some of the tension begin to leave her.

She might dislike Piers Morrison, but he had a knack of hitting the nail on the head.

She was spoiled, he was right, and she had never had to fight for anything in her life before. She was soft. And so were all those so-called friends of hers who seemed to spend their entire lives going to parties.

She squeezed her eyes shut tightly, feeling the sting of tears behind her eyelids. She knew that her father did not exactly approve of her lifestyle, but he had refrained from saying anything to her because he doted on her. And hadn't she taken advantage of that fact just a tiny bit? The realisation made her shudder with guilt.

She walked across to the little window, peeping over the magnificent panorama of blue sea and naked, craggy rocks, every detail sharp under the brilliant sunshine.

She thought about her fiancé Jonathan, Jonathan Whalley, who worked intermittently in his father's firm and spent the rest of the time playing hard.

Her father disapproved of him, and had said so, but she had always thought that he would come round to her point of view.

Now she wasn't even sure what her point of view was. Over the past three weeks her perspective on everything had been shifting, and that included her fiancé.

She had thought she loved him, and that he loved her, but now she wondered whether the only people they were capable of loving were themselves.

A tear trickled miserably down her cheek and she wiped it away with her fist.

Tears weren't going to solve anything at all. There was no point being weepy and maudlin. That wouldn't help her thinking at all, and wasn't that why she was here? To think?

She had a blurry image of Piers's face and started. He shouldn't be in her thoughts at all, and yet she found that in the short space of time since she had met him he had sunk in, wormed his way into her mind with his disturbing home truths.

What would he think of Jonathan?

Her friends all thought that theirs was a match made in heaven, the union of two gilded human beings. They even looked slightly alike, both with their fair, fair hair, except that Jonathan's eyes were blue, while hers were almost black.

They would be staggered when the engagement was broken off, and suddenly Alyssia found herself not caring overmuch for their reaction.

If only Jonathan had been around she might never have come to France, she might have stayed in London to explain it all to him, but he was away on business for a week, and the need to escape had been too powerful to resist.

Where better than the south of France, which she knew like the back of her hand? Jonathan's father owned a villa close to St Tropez, and she and Jonathan had toured the area extensively with friends.

She unpacked her cases, noticing the exquisite detail on all the fittings, and had a quick shower, slipping into a pair of flowered shorts, which showed off the length of her legs, and a halter top.

The smells wafting up the stairs from the kitchen were making her stomach churn, and she ran down, taking them two by two.

Piers was standing in the small kitchen, dwarfing it with his presence. He didn't look around when she came in, but asked her over the sizzling of bacon whether she wanted anything to drink.

'Umm,' Alyssia said, 'I'll have something long and cold.'

She waited, until he turned to face her.

'Something long and cool is in the fridge. You've got two legs that can carry you there and two hands that can pour it into a glass. In case it's missed you, this isn't a restaurant.'

He turned back to the frying-pan, and she wondered how anyone could make her hackles rise with so few words.

'And pour me one too, would you?' he added as she poured a glass of lemonade for herself, with lots of ice. 'Oh, and one more thing.'

I might have guessed, she thought tightly. 'Yes?'

'While you're here I'll expect you to do your share of the cooking. I have no intention of being chief cook and bottle-washer for the fortnight that you're around.'

He ladled a heaped portion of bacon on to their plates, quickly followed by cheese omelette and some crusty French bread.

Alyssia frowned. 'No one asked you to be,' she said stiffly, watching him slide his body into the chair and dig into his plate of food with relish.

'No,' he agreed, 'but I thought I'd just say so in case you got the wrong idea.' He was breaking the French stick, his eyes roving dispassionately over her scantily clad body, and she felt herself blush.

She was normally so cool and in command in the presence of men, but he made her feel gauche. And stirred something in her that was vaguely disturbing.

'Delicious,' she muttered, realising how hungry she was after the hours spent travelling.

'You can cook the dinner,' he informed her. 'There are some steaks in the freezer, and lots of vegetables.'

'Steaks? Vegetables?' She looked at him with a feeling of panic. 'What am I supposed to do with them? I can't cook.'

Complicated and delicious meals had always found their way to the table, and she had enjoyed them without ever bothering to find out how they were concocted.

Piers wiped his mouth with the napkin and relaxed back in the chair, surveying her through dark, thick lashes.

'Well, consider this the ideal time to learn,' he said softly, and she could have quite willingly screamed.

'I've never had to cook in my life before,' she muttered.

'No, I don't suppose you have. I've met types like you before. Quite content to have it all brought to you on a silver platter.'

'Don't you ever stop being rude?'

'I think you're confusing being rude with being truthful.'

'And I suppose you like your women hearty and full

of useful tips on cooking and gardening? One of those great Amazonian types who can do most things better than most other people?'

'Do I strike you as the sort of man who's attracted to Amazons?' he asked, his grey eyes flicking curiously on her face, waiting to hear what she would say, but, she felt, not terribly concerned whether she replied or not.

For some reason the thought that he seriously didn't care one way or another what her opinions were wounded her pride more than she would ever have admitted in a million years.

'Actually,' she said icily, 'I don't really care what sort of women you're attracted to. What mystifies me is that any woman could be attracted to you at all. You're insufferable.'

Ever as she said it, looking at him, at his finely tuned, muscular body and the sharp, clever, mocking planes of his face, she realised that he was sexually very attractive. To some women, she qualified to herself.

'Only to you,' he replied equably, 'and only because I don't fall in with what you want. Is that how most men react to you? Or should I say boys, because you don't strike me as ever having come into contact with any men.'

Alyssia bristled with rage. She tossed her hair back and addressed him levelly, keeping her rage in check. She was good at hiding her emotions and she did her utmost to now avail herself of the talent.

'How interesting that after only a few hours you know so much about me. You're wasted as a carpenter, or whatever it is you like to call yourself. And, for your information, my life isn't chock-full of boys, as you seem to imply——' not at the moment, anyway, she thought '—I happen to be engaged to just the one.'

She had been determined not to give anything of herself away to him, but he had succeeded in antagonising her to such a pitch that she almost couldn't help herself.

He clasped his hands behind his head and scrutinised her. 'I see,' he said thoughtfully.

'I doubt it.' This conversation was getting them both precisely nowhere, and, besides, it was making her feel uncomfortable. She wasn't used to expressing such volatility in front of anyone, and it confounded her how a total stranger, and a man she disliked into the bargain, was able to stir her to such an extent.

She stood up and began clearing the dishes away from the table, dumping them in the sink and then hurriedly washing them in some soapy water.

'What are your plans for the rest of the afternoon?' she asked in her best trying-to-be-friendly voice, thinking that if she could pin-point him to some specific part of the house then she could at least do her best to avoid it.

She could feel his eyes on her, and her body automatically tensed.

'Nothing that need concern you. After all,' he said lazily, 'I am only the carpenter.'

Alyssia glanced sharply at him. Had he known what she was thinking? It very much sounded so.

It also very much sounded as though he knew something she didn't, which was not a situation she liked. When it came to other people, particularly men, she preferred to be in control.

She frowned slightly. The astrologer had told her to beware of. . .no, surely not. The line of thought eluded her, but she remembered something else that had been said. Something to do with her desire to run things around her. Was that why she found the men in her life all so boring? Because they pandered to her? You're being over-imaginative, she told herself. Stick to reality and forget the stars.

'And what about you?' Piers asked, breaking into her thoughts. 'Will you go down to the beach? It's very private. You should be able to do quite a bit of useful contemplation about whether you actually love this boyfriend of yours.'

'What?' She turned to face him, staring into the grey eyes, thinking that, up close, he really was confusingly overpowering. 'You don't seem to have much hesitation about speaking your mind, whether I want to hear what's on it or not, so I'll speak mine for a change. My private life is absolutely none of your business whatsoever, and I'll thank you to keep your little pearls of insight to yourself.'

'Dear, dear, your highness,' he drawled with no attempt to hide the sarcasm in his voice, 'did I hit a soft spot?'

'No,' Alyssia very nearly shouted, 'you did not! And, if you don't mind, I think I'll go down to the beach now.'

Her face felt hot and flushed as she broke away from the magnetic pull of his eyes.

She walked quickly towards the door, throwing over her shoulder, 'At least I should be able to get some peace there.'

She flounced out of the kitchen, her normal poise and learned elegance deserting her for a moment, and quicky changed into her bikini in the bedroom, her mind buzzing with thoughts of Piers Morrison, and none of them very pleasant.

She made her way down the steep path to the cove,

ignoring the house entirely, still feeling angry at his insufferable high-handedness. She would have to have a word with her father about this man and find out what on earth had inspired him to hire him in the first place. Yes, as soon as she was through sunbathing she would amble into the village, which she knew reasonably well, and she would use the public phone box to get in touch with her father. Lord only knew when the telephone was going to be installed in the house, but if that man thought that he could speak to her however he wanted, safe in the knowledge that she was incommunicado, then he had another think coming.

She spread the towel flat on the sand and looked around her. Beautiful and peaceful. Crisp colours of blue and green, and the stark black of the rocks, and a pleasant breeze that made her feel slightly sleepy.

Normally, when she had visited the south of France with Jonathan, or with her friends, they had headed straight for the action. The trendy clubs, the casinos, where the women all dripped with gold and diamonds. How delicious, she thought, to be away from it all.

She dozed and woke, dozed and woke and finally fell into a light sleep, only stirring when she heard a voice addressing her from what seemed like a million miles away.

'You're heading for a bad attack of sunburn.'

Alyssia sat up quickly and looked at Piers, who was staring at her with that perpetual look of lazy mockery on his face. As though she were a species apart, and not a particularly pleasant one.

'What are you doing here?' she asked ungraciously, drawing her sun-wrap around her.

Normally she was not at all shy about her body. She was tall, perfectly proportioned, and was more than happy for it to be admired, just so long as the admiration did not get too intrusive.

With Piers it was different. He unsettled her. Under those impenetrable grey eyes, she felt awkwardly unclothed in her skimpy bikini, which allowed the maximum room for the sun and the minimum for coverage.

'What does it look like?' he asked with feigned surprise. 'I'm here to enjoy the sun.' He looked at her blandly. 'There's no need to cover yourself, you know.'

'I was doing no such thing!' she lied hotly.

'Weren't you? Anyway, you don't strike me as the sort who's ashamed of her body.'

'I'm not!' She looked at him suspiciously. 'And what does that remark mean, anyway?' She wanted dearly to inform him in no uncertain terms that he was in no position to make personal remarks of any kind to her, but she had an uneasy suspicion that any further rebukes on that score would only somehow backfire on her.

Piers lay down flat on his towel, pulling an old cap over his eyes. He was wearing a pair of olive-green bathing trunks, and nothing else. Alyssia's eyes roamed over his body, lean and muscled, and bronzed, as though he had spent a lot of time in the sunshine. Perhaps he had. She didn't know the first thing about him, after all. He might well live in the south of France, for all she knew.

It was rude to stare, she knew that much. It was something she never, ever did. But she found that she could not tear her eyes away from him. Brute strength, she thought disgustedly. That was it, of course. The attraction of brute strength.

The world was littered with men with muscles. Personally she had never been attracted to that sort in her life before. In truth, she rarely came across them. The boys in her group were almost all rather pampered-looking.

It baffled her as to why she should feel a tingle in her veins just because Piers Morrison was lying only a few inches away from her.

She shifted away slightly and repeated, 'What did your remark mean?'

'Remark?' Piers propped himself on his elbow and stared at her.

'Yes, remark. You know perfectly well what I'm talking about, so you can wipe that phoney puzzled look off your face.'

He pulled the cap a little lower to shield his eyes from the glare, and said negligently, 'I didn't think it needed explaining. As I said, you don't strike me as the sort of girl who hides her body from the public gaze, so I don't know why you're bothering to do so now.'

'I didn't think I was,' she said stiffly, sincerely hoping that he would swim out to sea and forget his way back.

'There's really no need,' he carried on, as though she hadn't spoken. 'I'm not interested in you sexually at all, you know. You're not my type.'

Alyssia's mouth fell open. No man had ever said that to her before. No man had probably ever even thought it. She was beautiful. Everyone told her so. She had basked in the knowledge for as long as she could remember.

His words dented her pride and left her speechless.

'Good,' she recovered quickly, 'the feeling's mutual.'

She stood up, and walked serenely down to the sea, holding her head high and thinking that she wasn't sure she could endure another thirteen days in the company of this man. She wasn't sure she could endure another thirteen *minutes* in the company of this man.

She ducked under the water, gasping as the cold hit her flesh. She persevered until gradually her body adjusted to the temperature, and then she really enjoyed herself, splashing around, not caring what sort of picture she presented.

When she walked back to her towel Piers had fallen asleep, and was snoring softly, the cap still pulled down over his face.

Brute, she thought acidly. Then she picked up the tall glass she had carried down with her, and which was now empty, walked sedately to the water's edge, filled it with ice-cold water and returned to see that he had not shifted.

She carefully tilted his cap back, held the glass about one foot over him and poured.

He spluttered back into life, sitting up abruptly, still addled by the suddenness of her action.

'There,' she said sweetly, relishing every word of her parting shot. 'We wouldn't want you to get sunburnt, now, would we?'

A sense of self-preservation cautioned her not to stick around, and before he could react she sprinted up to the house, feeling strangely exhilarated for the first time since she had left England.

CHAPTER TWO

ALYSSIA was still feeling inordinately pleased with herself when, half an hour later, she picked up the telephone in the little village post office and dialled her father's direct work line. She was one of the few who possessed it. Usually clients and business acquaintances went through his secretary, and only the very important calls got passed through.

At fifty-three, her father was still an intensely busy man, head of an important software company, and lately dabbling in property speculation. He had the personality for it, strong, aggressive and with an eye to a bargain.

Very few people ever saw his softer side, and she was one of them. He had lavished all his love on her, more so since her mother had died almost eighteen years ago, and, similarly, he was the only one who ever saw her vulnerable side.

Not even Jonathan, she thought suddenly, ever really saw anything but the smooth, exquisite façade that she presented to the outside world.

The telephone rang a few times, and then her father answered in his clipped, business-like voice.

'Dad,' she said, smiling, 'it's me. No need for the phone voice.' Now to sort this mess out.

She could almost feel him smiling down the line. 'Arrived safely, then?' he asked. 'How's the weather? It's awful over here—you're not missing much. Constant rain, and when it's not raining it looks as if it's about to. Typical English weather.' He chuckled softly.

26

'The weather's fine,' she said quickly. She had more important things to discuss than the weather. 'Dad,' she accused, 'you never told me that I would be sharing the house with some carpenter.'

'Carpenter?' her father asked with a tinge of bewilderment in his voice.

'Yes, carpenter. One Piers Morrison, to be precise.'

'Did he tell you that he was a carpenter?' He sounded amused. 'He's not a carpenter, dear, he's an architect, and a highly respected one at that. He's doing the house as a special favour to me.'

'Really,' Alyssia said, refusing to be impressed. 'Well, can't you persuade him to do it when I'm not around? He's the most unbearable human being I've ever met in my entire life——'

'Afraid not, darling,' her father interrupted. 'As I've said, he's been working off and on on the house as a favour. I can't very well ask him to take a fortnight off because you don't like him. Anyway, he's not in my employ. I'm surprised that he let you believe he was. As a matter of fact, he owns one of the largest and most innovative architectural companies in Europe. Normally he wouldn't touch a job as small as the cottage, but I once did a favour for his father, and when I mentioned that I was having trouble finding someone to do the job he volunteered.'

'But, Dad,' she protested desperately, 'I——'

'In fact,' her father cut in, 'if anything, I ought to be asking you to make sure that you don't antagonise him. Purely from a financial perspective, have you any idea how much more valuable the cottage will be when it's known to be one of Piers's creations?'

'Not antagonise him!' Alyssia exploded. 'He antagonises me! He doesn't know the meaning of the word "polite". I don't care if he's rich and famous!'

'Good lord!' her father said. 'Darling, I must dash, I'm late for a meeting. I love you, and take care.'

Alyssia was left holding the telephone receiver, hearing the dull dialling tone.

She replaced it with a frustrated sigh. So she had jumped to a few incorrect conclusions about Piers.

But the thought didn't make her any happier. She still didn't like him, she still didn't want to have him around, and now, from what her father had said, she hadn't got much option. She was stuck with him and his infuriating know-it-all attitude for the duration of her stay.

She bought a few bits and pieces from the post office and was feeling thoroughly deflated by the time she got back to the house.

To make matters worse, Piers was standing by the door when she returned, half naked, his T-shirt tied loosely around his waist, chiselling meticulously at the door-frame.

He looked up at her.

'Called your father?' he asked politely.

'Yes,' Alyssia snapped, 'as a matter of fact, I did.' She stood well away from him, doing her utmost to register distaste in her black eyes. No point in his getting any ideas that this was a bed of roses for her. She didn't care for him, and she had no intention of hiding the fact.

He turned back to what he was doing, his long fingers working quickly and expertly at the job, and she had the faintest feeling that she was being dismissed.

It wasn't a feeling that she liked.

'Why did you give me the impression that you were one of my father's employees?' she questioned without preamble.

'You gave yourself that impression,' he commented, without bothering to look at her. 'I merely saw no need to rectify it.'

'What do you mean by that?'

'What I mean, my girl, is that you swanned in here, full of self-righteous anger because a little carpenter had deigned to clutter your space without first consulting you, and quite frankly I was sick to my back teeth with what I saw.'

Alyssia's eyes widened.

He stopped chiselling and looked down at her. She felt suddenly giddy.

'I've taken the steaks out of the freezer,' he said, returning to his efforts with the door. 'In this weather they should more or less be thawed out. Don't let me stop you from beginning dinner.'

Alyssia placed her hands on her hips and glared at his back. She had been dismissed! *She*! For heaven's sake, she was the one who was accustomed to doing the dismissing!

She felt her eyes burn. She wanted to scream at him that she was nothing like that at all, but wasn't she? Hadn't she always concentrated all her energies on having a good time, even though she knew deep down that she wanted to do more with her life? She had toyed with the idea of doing volunteer work with the homeless, but had done nothing about it. Because, she acknowledged, I'm a coward.

She had the insane desire to tell all that to this man, but she bit back the words. If he hated her then let him. She didn't much care for him either!

So instead she stormed into the kitchen, surveyed the two lumps of meat and the assortment of vegetables, threw them all into the largest pot she could lay her hands on, and fried them. The vegetables took longer than she had expected, but by the time the table had been set they felt reasonably cooked.

She placed them in a casserole dish and then shouted for Piers to come inside and eat.

'Time for a shower?' he asked, wiping his brow with the back of one sweaty hand.

'That might be a good idea,' she said in a honeyed voice. 'Sweaty smells are always best left outside. We don't want you drowning out the aroma of the food, do we?'

Unexpectedly he laughed, long and loud, throwing his head back. With that cool, watchful look no longer on his face, she found that there was a certain appeal about him.

Almost sexy, she found herself thinking. If, she amended to herself, you went in for his type.

Except it struck her: what was his type? He had the body of an athlete, every sinew honed down to perfection, but he wasn't brainless. She knew that now, had known it from the very first moment she had met him, however more comfortable it would have been to dismiss him as all brawn and no brain.

She heard the sound of his footsteps upstairs, and then the more distant noise of the shower being turned on, and she resolutely shut her mind to any wayward thoughts that might arise from there.

She was determined that, at all costs, she would make sure he didn't ruffle her feathers again. She would be distant but polite.

By the time he re-emerged she felt in perfect control of everything. Her life, her thoughts, her emotions, the meal.

He lifted the cover of the casserole and sniffed.

'What is it?' he asked.

Her perfect control slipped a little. 'What does it

look like?' she replied briefly, beginning to dish her portion on to her plate and remembering the distant-but-polite motto.

'I can't begin to say.' He was staring at the concoction with open curiosity, as though trying to determine which category of plant, animal or thing it fell into. 'It's like nothing I've ever laid eyes on before.'

Alyssia stared defiantly into the dish, seeing the jumbled mass of vegetables, punctuated with two huge slabs of meat.

'Well, what did you expect?' she bit out, 'I told you I'd never cooked before! I'm hardly up to whipping out gourmet meals! If you want gourmet cooking you could always scout around in the village and see what you can get! Or else,' she added sourly. 'I'm sure there's some willing and able village lass dying to do your cooking for you. Why don't you get her to come over?'

He looked just the sort of hulk who would attract simpering village lasses.

'I thought I went for the Amazonian types,' he commented, ladling some of the food on to his plate warily.

'Who knows, and who cares.'

'Anyway, if I did have a village lass dying to do my cooking, don't you think she might find you a bit off-putting?'

Alyssia ignored his remark and concentrated on trying to cut her steak without sending all the vegetables flying at the same time.

'Actually, it was a joke. Though, to be frank, I couldn't care less if you had a hundred village lasses, all queueing up to do your cooking, cleaning and dirty-sock-washing. I have more important things on my mind.' At last. Success. She had managed to cut a piece of the steak into a biteable size. She chewed on

it and thought that it couldn't possibly be as rubbery as
it seemed.

'Oh, yes, forgot.'

Alyssia glanced up at him, disliking him even more
than she would have imagined possible. She pushed
the plate away from her, and said cuttingly, 'This is
awful. We'll have to get someone in to do the cooking.'

Piers abandoned his efforts with the meal and looked
at her with raised eyebrows.

'You believe in throwing your money about, don't
you?' he said, his voice dangerously soft. 'You've got
far too much for a girl of your age——'

'I'm twenty-two!'

'As I was saying, you've got far too much for a girl
of your age. And I'll be frank with you. . .'

'Go ahead. You've excelled at it so far.'

'. . .I've never heard such a ridiculous idea in my
entire life. Get someone in to do the cooking? In case
it's escaped you, this isn't London. This is a small
French village. Catering services do not exist at the
beck and call of an immature, over-wealthy child.'

'And how old are you?' she threw out.

'Me? In years, ten years older than you. In experience, about three hundred.'

He leaned back in his chair and surveyed her through
narrowed eyes.

Alyssia fiddled with the cutlery, feeling totally humiliated, though she had no intention of showing it. Her
remark had been in bad taste, she acknowledged, but
that was no reason for him to lay into her with yet
another string of personal insults, all dished out in that
patronising way that got her blood heated to boiing-
point. How dared he call her a child? Children, she
thought, didn't get engaged.

She thought of Jonathan, but decided that she must

have been too angry and hurt, because she could only manage to summon up the blurriest of images of him.

'I'm going into the village to see what I can find to eat. You can tag along if you want.'

Alyssia stood up haughtily. She would have liked to refuse his offer, she really would, but her stomach was growling with hunger and the thought of nothing in it till the morning was more than she could bear.

'You're too kind,' she muttered, following him to the door.

Outside the air had cooled slightly. Everything was bathed in a faded golden glow, and the only noises to be heard were the rustle of trees, the birds, and the occasional car chugging past.

She walked a little distance away from him, watching him out of the corner of her eye. Everything about him spelt self-assurance, the confidence of someone who had nothing at all to prove to the world.

'My father says that you're an architect,' she volunteered, determined to be pleasant even if it killed her in the process.

'I am,' Piers agreed, 'although you can continue to think of me as a glorified carpenter if you like.'

'I've never met any architects before,' she said, ignoring his gibe.

'Haven't you?' He looked across at her. 'No, I don't suppose your circle of friends would include any architects. What sort of people do you normally mix with?'

'The normal sort,' she replied, wondering why his most innocent of remarks had the power to antagonise her.

'Tell me, what does a rich young girl like you call the normal sort?' There was an edge to his comment that left her in no doubt that everything she said only confirmed the opinion he already had of her. A low one.

'Two legs,' she responded tartly, 'two arms, both in the right places. People who know how to enjoy themselves.' Her tone implied that he didn't, and it was just what she had intended.

'What do you do to enjoy yourself?' he asked incuriously.

'Oh, parties, clubs, nothing that you would know about, since you're three hundred years older than me.'

There was the vaguest notion of a smile on his lips, and she tightened her mouth.

'I get the picture,' he said.

'Oh, do you?' Alyssia stopped in her tracks, her hands on her hips. 'And what picture is it that you get? I might as well ask, because I suppose you'll tell me anyway.' She stood still and stared at him, the breeze whipping her long fair hair around her face, coiling it about her neck like strands of fine silk.

Piers took a step towards her, and she felt her body tense and her heart begin to beat quickly.

There really was something distinctly unsettling about this man, she thought. She had watched him working delicately on the door, with all the attention to detail of the perfectionist, and had known him to be the sort who got what he wanted in life through hard work, never by taking the easy way out.

She took a few deep breaths and told herself that she could handle him. Hadn't she always been able to handle the opposite sex? She was rich and she was beautiful, a strong combination. And she was totally self-confident. No one had ever been able to knock her for six, and if this man affected her at all it was because she disliked him so much.

'Well, now that you ask,' he said smoothly, 'the picture I get is of a group of young people with more money than sense, buying temporary pleasures because they haven't got a clue where to find enjoyment of the more permanent sort.'

'Really?' Alyssia said tightly. She began walking ahead quickly, and Piers kept up with her with long, easy strides.

I hate this man, she thought hotly. I hate him, I loathe him; he never says anything nice to me. It was an effort to force her features into a perfectly controlled smile.

'And I suppose,' she said disdainfully, 'that I should be impressed, since, of course, you are the guardian of the whole world's wisdom. Architect, philosopher, chef—what next? Dab hand on the violin and speaker of ten tongues?'

She glanced at him and saw his shoulders shaking. He was laughing at her!

'I'm glad you find me so hilarious!'

'You have to have some saving grace.'

'Which is more than I can say about you!'

'Really?' He turned to face her, and, in the half-light, the sexuality of his face was even more pronounced. 'I haven't had too many complaints.'

There was no response to that. It conjured up too many graphic images for her to reply with any semblance of iciness.

'We're here,' she managed to mutter, even though her mouth felt like sandpaper.

They were standing outside a small bistro. She hadn't even noticed when they reached the village. She ran her fingers through her hair and tried to ignore his presence alongside her.

When he touched her on her elbow to guide her

inside she very nearly snatched her arm away, only controlling the impulse at the last minute. His hand could only have been on her for a matter of seconds, if that, but when he released her she felt as though her skin had been scorched

The proprietor must have thought that they were lovers because he showed them to the most secluded table in the place, talking all the while in rapid French, which she couldn't understand at all, but which Piers had no trouble in comprehending. He nodded and replied, also in rapid French, and Alyssia wondered whether her quip about the ten tongues was nearer the truth than she had imagined.

'You speak French,' she said neutrally, thinking, I might have guessed.

Piers nodded, ordering both their meals. 'I'm bilingual. My mother was French. I began my first job in France. Now I do nearly everything from London, and delegate most of the rest.'

'Why did you leave?'

'That,' he replied abruptly, 'is none of your business.'

A shutter came down over his eyes and she had the sensation of having had a door slam very firmly in her face.

The proprietor brought them their plates heaped with beef and wild mushrooms and bordered with vegetables, breaking the silence between them.

When he next spoke it was about something trivial, and Alyssia replied in the same vein, stifling the burning curiosity to find out what dark secrets he was keeping behind that controlled face of his.

After all, didn't everyone have their secrets?

Of course, she thought, she didn't really care, but

wasn't it natural that she should be curious about him? He was so unlike anyone she had ever met.

'Why are you here?' she asked when she had finished eating her meal and was sipping from her cup of coffee. 'I mean, why are you doing this for Dad? I know he told me that it was some sort of favour for something he did for your father a long time ago, but what?'

He looked at her from under those thick dark lashes, as though contemplating whether to answer her question or not.

'He bailed my father out of some financial difficulty a long time ago,' he said shortly.

'And so you're repaying the favour after all these years?'

Piers shrugged. 'I never forget my debts. In fact, I never forget anything.'

There was a hard undercurrent in his voice, as though he was almost unaware of her existence, as though he was thinking aloud, and referring to something specific, although she had no idea what.

Then his eyes refocused on her, and that brief feeling of hovering on the brink of something important vanished.

'You've returned,' she said with a hesitant smile.

'Returned?'

'To planet earth. For a moment there you seemed to be miles away. I wondered what was going through your head.'

'Did you, now?' he said in a voice of steel. 'Take my advice; leave your curiosity for your breed of friends. As far as I'm concerned, it could be a dangerous indulgence.'

The barriers between them were back in place. She felt herself bristle at his tone of voice. He was warning her off! Most men would have been flattered by her interest, and he was warning her off! Did he think that her curiosity was leading up to something? If so, he couldn't be further from the truth. For starters, she had enough on her plate with Jonathan and her disillusionment with him, and, for a second thing, she was as uninterested in him as he was in her.

She glared at him, wondering whether the indigestible steak, swiftly followed by an early night, might not have been a better option after all.

'Don't worry,' she said coldly, 'I think you were confusing politeness with curiosity. Personally I couldn't give a damn about your private life.'

'Good. Just so long as we understand each other.'

'Oh, believe me, we do. You don't want me to intrude on your territory.'

'Precisely.'

'Does anyone?' she caught herself saying rashly. Her question seemed to catch her more off guard than it did him, and she felt a warm blush rise to her cheeks.

It didn't matter to her, did it, so why, then, was she pursuing this like a dog with a bone? They had been thrown together as strangers, and so they would remain. She didn't even exist in the equation, since, as far as he was concerned, she was little more than a child. That he had said, quite bluntly.

'I think it's time we left,' she muttered, standing up and thereby giving him no opportunity to deliver another of his pointed snubs.

'I think you're probably right.'

When she fished inside her bag for her wallet he shook his head.

'No woman ever pays when she's with me.'

Alyssia looked at him in surprise, although his remark wasn't totally unexpected.

It wasn't often that men shrugged off her attempts to

pay her way. They knew that she had money, and most of them saw no reason why they shouldn't go Dutch when they went out, and, until now, neither had she.

Only Jonathan had no qualms about paying for her wherever they went, but maybe that was because he was as rich as she was, even if it was all his father's money.

Wasn't that what had attracted her to him in the first place? The safety of knowing that at least he wasn't after her for her father's wealth? As quite a handful of her boyfriends had been?

They walked back to the house in silence. There was a heady scent of rosemary and thyme in the air, and she breathed it in, feeling strangely at peace for the first time in as long as she could remember. There were no distractions here. No loud music, or bright lights, or chattering voices.

Just, of course, Piers Morrison, but, she decided, he was more of an inconvenience than a distraction.

Men had only ever been pleasant pastimes in her full and varied life. She liked it that way, and she intended keeping it that way. Her engagement had been a bitter mistake, but it had at least taught her a lesson in preserving her invulnerability, instead of charging into things with unbridled optimism.

Meantime, civilisation seemed like light-years away. Her old self would have seemed like light-years away as well if Mr Know-it-all didn't keep reminding her that it wasn't.

She looked at him, stumbled, tripped and fell.

Nothing soft to cushion the fall. She felt a burning on her knee and grimaced.

Piers was bending over her, and she felt him helping her up.

'I'm fine,' she managed to get out, gritting her teeth against the raw pain in her foot.

She made an attempt to pull herself out of his reach. A futile gesture, as he lifted her off the ground, and before she could react she was being carried unceremoniously to the house.

'I'm fine. Really.' She tugged away, and he held her tighter.

'I'll have a look at that when I get to the house.'

'You're not a doctor as well, are you?' Hardly the most appropriate thing to say when he was helping her, but she had to say something, anything, to hide her flustered response to being this close to him. And she was close. She could hear his heart thudding under her ear, feel his warmth pressed against her, making her giddy.

She vainly pleaded to be let down, so that she could hobble back to the house with some semblance of dignity, and he steadfastly ignored all her pleas.

By the time they made it back to the house she no longer knew whether she was as fine as she had insisted on telling him. Her head was swimming and her heart was pounding.

He awkwardly unlocked the door and carried her to the sofa, laying her down as though she weighed nothing at all.

'Now, let's have a look.' He shifted the hem of her dress above her knee and Alyssia stiffened.

'I know a bit about first aid,' she protested weakly. 'If you could just get me some warm water I——'

'Will you stop acting as though I'm going to rape you,' he said impatiently. 'Stay put, I'll be back in a sec.'

He headed off in the direction of the kitchen, and she made a feeble effort to straighten her leg, wincing in pain. It was nothing serious, she knew that, just a bad bruise in need of cleaning, and the last person in the world she wanted to do the cleaning was him.

He returned carrying some tepid water and cleaning material, and gently began wiping the sore cut.

Alyssia tried to remain cool, calm and collected, watching him as his long fingers worked away. Inside she was a jumble of emotions, none of them reasonable.

Those hands, she thought, one resting lightly on her thigh while the other cleaned the wound. What would they feel like on other parts of her body?

The mere thought shocked her and she jerked back.

Piers looked up in surprise. 'That hurt?'

'No,' she mumbled, scarlet-faced. 'Yes!'

'All done. That wasn't too bad, was it?' The grey eyes rested a fraction too long on her face, then he said, 'Shall I kiss it better?'

This time Alyssia really did pull away, and he laughed under his breath. 'Joke,' he said softly.

He strolled back into the kitchen and she glowered at his departing back. Some joke. It didn't strike her as the slightest bit funny.

He didn't mind telling her in no uncertain terms to keep her distance from him, not that she had any inclination to do anything else, but obviously felt no compulsion to obey those rules when applied to himself.

When she thought she was about to explode she stormed up the stairs, slamming her bedroom door shut behind her and leaning heavily against it.

The man really was the limit. She couldn't believe that she had actually thought him human occasionally. She changed into her nightie, surprised at how late it was, still seething.

What on earth was happening to that girl she had left behind in London? The one who always seemed to have everything and everyone under control? She desperately wanted to retrieve her, but it was proving more and more elusive.

She slipped under the bedclothes and switched on the reading lamp, adamant that she would shove him to the furthest corner of her mind, but the minute she opened her book her brain started working again, throwing up images of him, the way he smiled, that confident knowing look in his eyes when he addressed her. As though he could see right into the deepest bits of her. Bits that she hadn't even known existed.

Jonathan never probed the way he did. They simply had a good time together without really asking too many questions about each other.

Maybe, she thought bitterly, if she had asked a few questions she might have uncovered the truth about him for herself, instead of having the information relayed to her by one of her friends. She had known deep down that he was a womaniser, but to think that their engagement meant so little to him that. . .

She stuffed her head into the pillow in pained anger.

She had run away, not something in keeping with her character at all, but she had done so nevertheless.

The question was, to what had she run?

Tomorrow would be another day, and she would make damned sure that she would get it off on the right footing. The long journey across, the shock of realising that she would have to share the house with a complete stranger, and a highly undesirable one at that, had disorientated her. In the morning she would be back to her normal self. And not a moment too soon.

She switched off the light, and waited in the silence, listening to the footsteps downstairs.

When, after an hour, she heard him coming up the stairs she pulled the sheets tightly around her, and then relaxed.

What was she afraid of? she thought with disgust. That he was going to barge into her bedroom and reveal some deeply untrustworthy side to his personality?

Hardly! He had already told her that she wasn't his type. That thought, she told herself, made her feel a lot better.

Besides, as far as he was concerned, she was engaged.

She was distracted by the sound of running water, the bath being filled.

Then she thought about Piers, seeing his nudity as he stepped into the bath with astounding clarity. She gasped at the vividness of her imagination.

Thank heaven that in the morning everything would be back to normal.

CHAPTER THREE

ALYSSIA had planned to spend the entire fortnight relaxing on the beach, drinking in the sun and getting gloriously tanned. She had planned, she thought as she warily made her way downstairs the following morning, on solitude.

Instead, here she was, creeping around her own house like a burglar, trying to avoid a man who rubbed her up the wrong way.

He was contemptuous of her, of her lifestyle, of her attitude, and he was arrogant enough to make no effort to conceal it. So much for relaxing on the beach, she thought. Relaxing in a snake pit would have been preferable. No, she would go into Nice. One of her closest friends—in fact, her closest friend—lived in Nice with her brother. She would call on them, and then she would spend the rest of the day shopping.

That way she could avoid Piers Morrison for hours on end. It was the ideal solution.

As luck would have it, he was standing at the kitchen counter, his back to her, making himself a sandwich. She looked at the tall, supple body and wondered whether he was ever polite to anyone. Was he even going to acknowledge her presence?

As if reading her mind, he said over his shoulder, 'There's coffee in the percolator. Pour us some, would you?'

'Good morning,' Alyssia said.

'Oh, good morning.'

'And doesn't the word "please" exist in your vocab-

44

ulary?' Nevertheless, she got up and poured two mugs of coffee and sipped hers. The coffee in France always seemed to be superior to the coffee in England, and he had made it just right. Not too strong and not over-weak.

'There's bread in the oven,' he informed her, without bothering to turn around.

She scowled at the broad back, with the T-shirt stretched taut over his muscles, and wondered how it would look with a sandwich hurled at it. Why was it, she wondered, that she couldn't even summon up the rudiments of politeness with this man?

'I don't normally eat breakfast at all,' Alyssia informed him, her mouth beginning to water at the smell. 'I can't afford to put on too much weight.'

He turned around and stared at her with that insuf-ferable thoroughness, which was downright rude, but about which she couldn't complain. How could she say that it made her feel uncomfortable?

'Why not?' he asked. 'You're much too thin. You could afford to put on a few pounds.'

'Not if I want to continue fitting into all my clothes.' Good grief, what century was this man living in? Did he think that the Rubenesque figure was still fashionable?

She bit into a croissant and tried unsuccessfully to ignore his presence.

'What are your plans for the day?' he asked, pre-paring another mammoth sandwich for himself. Where on earth did he store it? she wondered. There wasn't an ounce of surplus fat on his body, so it must go somewhere. Probably right to that big mouth of his.

'I thought,' she said, ignoring her father's advice to treat him with kid gloves, 'not that it's any business of yours, that I might potter into Nice for the day.'

'Beginning to pine for some excitement?'

'Beginning to pine for some relaxed company, if you must know. I have some friends there. I'm going to pay them a visit.'

'Fine, I'll take you. There are one or two things I need to get myself.'

'Take me?' She stared at him, aghast. 'I can take myself, thank you very much. And, besides, how would you take me anyway? On your back? I don't recall seeing any cars parked outside.'

'Oh, I have a car, all right. It's in the garage, a little further up the hill.'

An answer for everything, she thought.

'Well, there's no need. If you give me a list I can get whatever you need and bring it back with me.'

'We'll set off as soon as we've eaten. How's the knee?'

'The knee is fine, thank you.' And so was I, Alyssia thought, until I came downstairs.

'Good.' He was working his way through his food with astonishing speed. When he was finished he stood up and said to her, 'Leave your plate.' The grey eyes skimmed over her until she felt her face turning red. 'And run upstairs and change into something more suitable. You can meet me outside in ten minutes.'

She wanted to make some sarcastic retort about his being so bossy, but he was already clearing away the plates, not paying the slightest scrap of attention to her, and she realised that it was this lack of attention that really annoyed her.

She wasn't accustomed to it. She was always the centre of activity. People noticed her. It was vaguely insulting to know that he treated her as casually as he would have treated any stranger with whom he found himself forced to share a house.

She walked upstairs and changed quickly, slipping on a light flowered sundress in bold colours and her flat sandals.

Then she checked her appearance in the mirror, objectively staring back at the exquisite reflection, the shining flaxen hair, the huge dark eyes, the full mouth. She didn't look anything like a child, she thought.

He was waiting for her outside and they walked up the hill a little way; then she noticed the garage, stuck back a bit into the foliage, and the car inside it.

'This,' she said in horror, 'is a car?'

'How very observant,' he said drily.

Car, she thought, was a loose intrepretation. It had four wheels, but that was where the similarity to anything she had ever driven ended. It looked like some enormous battery-powered bug, and she had serious misgivings as to whether it would make it out of the garage, never mind to Nice.

The last thing she needed was to be trapped in a broken-down vehicle with Piers Morrison.

He drove it out of the garage, and she heard the high-pitched, wheezing motor with dread.

'Are you sure it's safe?' she asked, climbing inside, and screwing up her face at the simplicity of all the fittings. The seats were like upholstered benches, and God only knew how the gear-stick operated. One yank and she had a feeling it would detach itself completely from the dashboard.

'Quite safe.' He eased it on to the narrow road and it coughed and spluttered along. 'Not what you're used to?' he asked.

'Is anybody used to this?' She almost had to shout to drown out the noise of the engine.

'Oh, thousands of people,' Piers informed lazily.

'Cars don't begin and end with Porsches, believe it or not.'

'I know that!' Alyssia snapped. 'I'm just not used to something that looks as though it should have wings and be flying in the air instead of being driven!'

He laughed under his breath and looked at her with reluctant appreciation, but Alyssia didn't notice because she was staring out of the window at the passing scenery, keeping her fingers tightly crossed that the car wouldn't stop wheezing and die completely on them before they reached Nice.

It was a blessing that they didn't have very far to go, and the road was uncrowded.

She had been to Nice countless times. She knew it almost as well as she knew London. It was the sizzling unofficial capital of the Riviera, and she loved it because it was so alive. The shops were great, the restaurants were great, and the night-life was wonderful.

'Still awake?' Piers asked her.

'Of course I am!'

'Doing some thinking?'

'No,' Alyssia said in a honey-sweet voice, 'I wasn't doing some thinking. I was planning how I was going to spend the day!'

'I take it you've been here before.'

'Correct.'

'With your boyfriend?'

'Could you please concentrate on the road and on getting this tired old heap of metal there in one piece, instead of on matters that don't concern you?'

'I am getting heartily sick of your attitude, my girl.' His voice was laced with derision and Alyssia flushed guiltily, remembering her father's words. She should apologise, she knew that, but she wouldn't. She doubted the words would even be able to leave her mouth.

She stared straight ahead with unblinking concentration.

'What do you want to talk about, then?' she asked finally.

'What about Nice? It would be an infinitely less tiring topic than anything else.'

Was that boredom she could detect in his voice? The thought made her cringe.

'I don't know anything about it,' she admitted. 'I know I've been here loads of times before, but. . .'

'You never saw the need to take any interest in your surroundings,' he finished for her. 'True? Silly question, though, isn't it? Of course you didn't. Do you ever?'

Alyssia flushed, hating his tone of voice. It held distinct overtones of disgust.

'Not usually,' she said through pursed lips, wishing that she could somehow refute his image of her, 'and please, spare me another amateur lecture on my psyche. I don't know anything about the history of Nice because. . .'

'Because?'

Because, she thought, she had never been there with anyone who was interested in taking it at anything other than face value. They had accepted it for what it was, and never bothered to probe deeper, and she had followed suit.

They were driving into the city now, and she looked around her, seeing it with different eyes for the first time, seeing it as a garrulous old lady with so much to tell to anyone willing to listen.

'Could you drop me off here?' she asked quickly, blinking away the moment of self-analysis. The car was chugging along the Promenade des Anglais, a boulevard lined with splendid palm-trees. From here she would be able to make her way to the shopping areas, which were primarily reserved for pedestrian traffic.

Her friends, Simone and her brother André, owned a boutique that sold a combination of souvenirs for the tourists and handmade clothes.

The car pulled over, and Piers turned to her.

'Where shall I pick you up?'

'Oh, here will do. . .' she looked at her watch '. . .say, about four o'clock?' She plastered a polite smile on her face and turned the door-handle.

'What about lunch? Twelve o'clock outside the Normande café in the old quarter?'

'I have other plans,' Alyssia informed him flatly.

'What other plans?'

'Oh, for heaven's sake! We're slowing down the traffic!'

'What other plans?'

'I'm hoping to have lunch with a couple of friends of mine!'

'Good. I look forward to meeting them. Bring them along.'

'But——'

'Twelve sharp. And be prompt,' he told her, 'arriving late isn't a woman's prerogative, it's just rude. You'd better go now, we're slowing down the traffic.' He looked at her as if challenging her to argue with him and Alyssia had the drowning feeling of someone whose control had been very efficiently whipped out of her grasp.

Then he leaned across her and pushed open the door. Her protest died on her lips as his arms brushed across her breasts, and a fierce feeling of confusion swept over her.

'Twelve o'clock!' he called out as she stepped on to the pavement; then he was gone, the little green car melding into the rest of the traffic and rapidly becoming lost to sight.

So much for the escape, she thought ill-humouredly as she made her way to the boutique. Trying to escape him was about as feasible as trying to escape a very big shark in a very small fish tank.

She walked through the Jardin Albert-1er, with its picturesque fountain and outdoor theatre, and then plunged into the network of streets, all lined with their exquisite shops.

Simone's boutique was nestled in between a shoe shop and a jewellery shop. Alyssia hesitantly walked in, and almost immediately saw her friend by the cash register, looking with interest at a couple of oldish women who had put on some very garish dresses and were inspecting themselves in the mirror.

Suddenly she felt wonderfully happy. She didn't see Simone very often, but they had known each other from their schooldays and could pick up their friendship without the slightest difficulty.

She rushed up and threw her arms around her in a totally uncharacteristic gesture of affection, and felt all the stress of Piers Morrison lift from her shoulders as they began chatting animatedly about everything under the sun, catching up on old news.

Simone was one of those girls who hardly seemed to change at all from one year to the next. She had a plump, pretty face, framed by dark curls that resisted every effort at restraint. Quite different from her brother, who was slim where she was rotund, and whose dark hair lent him a certain swarthy, though boyish, kind of good looks.

He was nowhere to be seen.

'But he'll be around later,' Simone told her, 'and he'll be thrilled that you're here. You know how he fancies you.'

Alyssia nodded with a grin. She knew, all right. He had never made much pretence at hiding it. Simone had written to her shortly after her engagement had been announced to congratulate her, not omitting to mention that André had been shattered.

Alyssia had seriously doubted it. André was far too exuberant to be shattered by something like that, but it had given her ego a kick.

It might be quite nice seeing him now, she thought. Some harmless flirting, lots of compliments. Might make up for Piers Morrison.

They arranged to meet for lunch, and she said, 'But I might as well warn you, it won't be just the three of us. Piers Morrison, the man who's working on the house, will be there as well.'

'Piers Morrison.' Simone frowned slightly. 'Name rings a bell. Isn't he that architect?'

'You've heard of him?'

'Yes, I have. Quite a coup to have him working on your house, isn't it? What's he like?'

Alyssia felt faint. Was he that famous? Obviously.

She looked at her friend and wanted to ask whether she had a few days to spare, because that was how long any description of him would take. Instead she settled for the three most applicable adjectives she could think of. 'Arrogant, infuriating and objectionable.'

And some, she thought, as she resumed her shopping.

The clothes in the boutiques were as superb as always, and by eleven-thirty she had managed to accumulate an assortment of bags which were beginning to feel as though they weighed several tons instead of a few pounds.

She made her way to the old city, the Vieille Ville, with a certain amount of relief.

Normally when she came here she and her friends went directly to the restaurant of their choice. But now she looked around her, really seeing for the first time the humming activity of the fruit and vegetable market, breathing in the aromatic smells, noticing how charming the open square was, with its border of pizza stalls and cafés and bistros. Had she never noticed it before? She must have!

The restaurant where she had arranged to meet Piers was close to the Palais Lascaris, an old, breathtakingly beautiful town house, and she located it without too much difficulty.

She didn't much care whether she was early or late. She just needed relief from her burden of bags. She got herself seated at a table for four, ordered a glass of *pastis*, the local drink, and settled back to wait for her friends. And Piers.

As luck would have it, Piers was dead on time. He spotted her immediately and strolled across, stopping on the way to have a few words with the patron. How did he manage to make conversations with other people such light-hearted affairs, when it was such heavy going with her?

'You're on time,' he said, sitting in the chair opposite her, and calling the *garçon* across to order a drink.

Alyssia nodded. He had been carrying a small bag, which he dumped on the table, and she looked at it in disbelief.

'You mean you came all the way into Nice to get something that could be fitted into an envelope?' She succeeded in conveying through her voice an element of 'you mean you spoilt my day for something so trivial?' 'I could quite easily have picked it up for you. There was no need to drag yourself here.'

'Believe me, if I didn't want to come to Nice I wouldn't be here now.'

His beer arrived and he took one long sip from it, tilting his head back.

'Where's your friend?' he asked, relaxing in the chair, making it look far too small for someone of his length and muscularity.

'Friends,' Alyssia corrected, 'plural. Two of them. Simone and her brother André.'

She spotted them at the door and waved them over.

But she didn't feel relaxed at all. She was too conscious of Piers lounging in the chair opposite her to relax. Every muscle in her body felt attuned to his presence. Damned man.

She waited until Simone and André were seated, and then made the introductions.

André was on good form. He spent a few minutes making polite, nondescript conversation, then he proceeded to devote the remainder of the meal to Alyssia.

He was theatrical by nature, and he lavished it all on her, complimenting her in the most exuberant terms, telling her that her engagement had broken his heart irreparably.

She looked into his dark eyes and submerged herself in the bliss of being flattered.

It really was heartening, after her disenchantment with Jonathan, and after Piers.

Out of the corner of her eye she saw that he and Simone were getting along like a house on fire. He was being more than merely polite, he was being charming, the grey eyes glinting with warmth, the sensuous mouth parted in laughter.

What a creep, she thought. Anyone looking at the

two of them would think that they were lovers. So much for Simone believing her stories about him being insufferable.

When he excused himself to go to the bathroom Simone turned to her, her dark eyes shining.

'How could you say that he was arrogant?' she accused. 'He's the most charming man I've met in a long time.'

'About as charming as a bout of flu,' Alyssia muttered under her breath.

'And good-looking with it! Don't you find him attractive?'

'In a very basic sort of way,' Alyssia replied.

'Well, just as well,' Simone said; 'after all, you're engaged. I don't suppose you've got eyes for anyone but dear old Jonathan.'

Alyssia didn't ask her friend to explain the sarcasm in her voice. She knew that Simone didn't care much for Jonathan and she was willing to leave the subject alone.

'Where is he, anyway?' Simone asked.

Alyssia shrugged vaguely, knowing that this wasn't the time or the place to confide in her friend. 'Somewhere in Geneva. On business. His father sent him.'

'I didn't think for one minute that he'd made it there under his own steam,' Simone murmured, and André laughed smugly.

Why was she being victimised? Alyssia thought. First by Piers High-handed Morrison, and now by her closest friend.

She changed the subject, just as Piers sat back down, favouring Simone with a broad smile and herself with nothing at all.

Poor little rich girl. His remark flashed through her

head, stirring her anger, making her respond to André with much more warmth than she normally would have.

By the time they were ready to leave she was having to use every ounce of effort to convince André that no, she didn't want to paint the town red, or any other colour, for that matter, and no, she didn't want to have any candlelit dinners with him.

Finally she agreed to meet him for lunch the following week, and they agreed a time and a place.

All the while, Piers hovered in the background, not saying a word, like some dark, dangerous force that she could turn her back on but couldn't quite manage to ignore.

He remained silent as they walked back to the car and he opened the passenger-door for her.

'Nice girl, Simone,' he said casually as the car coughed its way into life.

'Mmm.'

'Known her long?'

Alyssia thought about it. How long? Must be at least ten years. 'A few years,' she said. 'We went to school together, and then Simone came out here about two years ago to open the boutique. Her parents are divorced and her mother lives with them.'

'She's unpretentious,' Piers commented, 'not what I had expected.'

'Meaning that any friend of mine is automatically going to be pretentious?'

He glanced across at her, then back at the road. 'You can interpret my remark any way you like.'

'And what,' she asked blandly, 'did you think of André?'

'Not a great deal, if you must know.'

'No,' Alyssia said, unable to resist the impulse to be

catty, 'men generally are a bit wary of him because he's so good-looking.'

'Do you think he's good-looking?'

The grey eyes shot across to her again, and Alyssia thought with shock that she didn't. Not nearly as good-looking as the man sitting right next to her. Oh, André was always a hit with the girls, and he did have a certain effeminate appeal and a wonderful way with words, but he lacked Piers's vitality, the vibrant sexuality that seemed to smoulder away inside him.

'Yes,' she said, 'as a matter of fact, I do.' She stared out of the window, disturbed. Her heart was beating quickly, making her feel out of breath. How on earth could she even think Piers sexy? Hadn't she had enough of men for the moment, without being stupid enough to allow herself the folly of being attracted to a man who couldn't basically give a damn whether she existed or not?

'And what would the boyfriend think of that?'

'I wish you'd stop referring to him as "the boyfriend". In fact, I don't see why you have to refer to him at all. Anyway, because I'm engaged it doesn't mean that I can't appreciate other men's attractiveness. It's not as if I'm going to run off and have affairs with them just because they're physically appealing.'

'Wouldn't you?'

'No, I would not! I admit that I find his attention flattering. What's so abnormal about that?' The colour had risen in her cheeks. 'Wouldn't you be flattered if a beautiful woman threw herself at you?'

'No,' he said in a hard voice, 'quite frankly I can't imagine anything more disgusting than a woman who drops all semblance of pride to run after a man.'

'I don't believe you!'

'And I don't give a damn what you believe.'

Alyssia flushed at the insult. Why was it that this man had the ability to bring tears to her eyes? God, how she loathed him.

And was he really trying to tell her that he really didn't indulge in casual affairs? Ha! Men always indulged in casual affairs if they could.

Just look at Jonathan, she thought bitterly.

No, he just didn't want her prying, seemed to have a thing about her treading too closely to his private life.

She revised her thoughts of Amazons and village maidens, though. He was so tall and masculine that he probably went for the dainty feminine types. The simpering sort who would do anything for him and knew how to knock up gourmet dinners in fifteen minutes flat.

'What are we going to eat tonight?' she asked, changing the subject rapidly because thoughts of Piers Morrison in bed with a simpering, dainty blonde made her feel uncomfortable. She looked at the strong hand as it shifted gears and continued resting on the lever. What bodies had those hands touched? Really?

'I've bought some stuff.' He motioned to the boot with a slight movement of his head. 'You can try your hand at cooking again when we get back. I should steer clear of the throw-it-all-in-a-pot philosophy, though. That only works when you know what you're doing.'

'Thank you so much for the advice,' Alyssia muttered, relieved that some of the tension had been dissolved. 'I personally think it's much easier just to have a meal out.'

Odious man. Where was all that charm he had lathered with sickening profuseness on Simone? Evaporated the minute they had parted company with her and André, that was for sure.

The heavy lunch and the wine had made her sleepy,

and she took to her bed the minute they returned, only awakening when the hunger pangs assaulted her stomach, to see that she had been asleep for over three hours.

She shot out of bed, hurriedly slipping on a pair of jeans and a sleeveless blue vest, against which the pale gold of her tan and the whiteness of her hair shimmered. She barely noticed it at all as she stood for a few seconds in front of the mirror and pulled the comb through her hair.

Then she rushed downstairs. She was hungry, there was food, and the sooner she did something with it, the sooner her appetite would be sated.

Piers was nowhere to be seen, and without his presence in the kitchen she thought carefully about what she was going to do with the bits of chicken and the assortment of vegetables.

He was right. Tossing it all together in a heap in a pan, and then hoping for the best, would produce another totally inedible meal.

She fried the chicken in some butter, put the vegetables on to boil, remembering the salt at the last minute, and was debating how to make a cheese sauce that bore some resemblance to those she had eaten in the past, when he walked in.

'Smells good. . .' he sniffed the air appreciatively, then looked into the frying-pan. . .'and, so far, still looks appetising.'

'Very amusing.'

'Can I do anything?' he asked.

'Do you know how to make a cheese sauce?'

'Of course I do.'

The wine had lowered her defences. She smiled at him, and said teasingly. 'Of course you do. How could

I forget that you know how to do most things, short of open-heart surgery?'

He laughed, and she found herself laughing with him, enjoying the moment, wanting it to continue.

He stood in front of the saucepan and instructed her, and she found herself obeying his orders, putting the butter in first, then melting it, stirring the flour in, and adding the milk slowly, then the cheese.

'You've got to stir it constantly,' he said. He circled her with his arms, forming a cage around her, and Alyssia felt her heart leap into her mouth. He was so close to her, his arms brushing lightly against hers, making her hairs stand on end. She could hardly concentrate on what he was doing, because she was far too busy concentrating on making sure that her stupid legs didn't crumble under her.

When he motioned for her to take the wooden spoon from him she did so, avoiding touching him at all costs.

She had no idea that any man could ever bring her out in goose-bumps, but this one had. He had made her whole body feel as though it would explode at the slightest caress from him.

Ridiculous, she told herself, relieved when he moved away to pour them both some Perrier water. But she had to shake her head to clear it of the dizzy sensation.

They ate outside. Piers had set up the garden table and two benches, and they had what turned out to be a very edible meal under the fading sun, with a magnificent view overlooking the still blue sea, with all the night noises playing a symphony around them. He had opened a bottle of wine, and Alyssia sipped cautiously from the glass, not wanting to lose control again because she was tipsy.

'Good,' he said when he had finished, closing his

knife and fork. 'A very creditable effort, considering you had to be forced into it.'

'Thank you very much,' she said, feeling disproportionately pleased at the compliment. Pleased and strangely girlish, which was a feeling she had not had in a very long time. 'You did help,' she added generously. 'Where did you learn to cook, anyway?'

'Usual place. In a kitchen.'

She giggled. 'You know what I mean.'

'I know what you mean. Believe it or not, bachelors do tend to cultivate the art, when it's a choice of either starving or else eating out every night, which can be very boring after a while. You'll have to cultivate it as well when you're married to the boyfriend.'

'Suppose so,' Alyssia murmured non-committally.

'And will you?'

'Will I what?'

'Marry him?'

He wasn't looking at her at all when he said this. His eyes were half closed as he drank from his glass, and there was a sudden stillness in the air as he waited for her reply.

She should have become angry with him for his persistence, on cue, but for some reason she didn't.

She twirled the stem of her wine glass thoughtfully, and didn't reply.

He was looking at her this time, directly into her eyes, and in the twilight she felt her pulses begin to race, and she thought, Oh, my God, I'm really attracted to this man.

She stood up abruptly, reaching out to take his plate.

'Leave it,' he said, taking hold of her wrist. 'You look as though you could do with some sleep.'

She didn't feel sleepy at all. Just the opposite. She felt keenly alert, her nerves on edge, but his offer gave her a reason to get out of being with him and of having to cope with her muddled feelings.

So she nodded in agreement, but he didn't release her wrist. Instead he stood, so that she had to gaze up to see his face.

'I am sleepy, now that you mention it.' She gave a little, nervous laugh, and then he lowered his head, and was kissing her, his lips moving lingeringly over hers, his tongue tracing patterns on her lips, probing the yielding softness of her mouth.

Alyssia moaned, her whole body responding to him. What was happening to her?

He grasped the back of her neck with his hand, and his kiss became fiercer, hungrier, until she thought that she was going to drown in it. She ran her trembling fingers through his hair, arching back as his lips found her neck and she felt the delicious sensation of his teeth, soft against her flesh.

When his hand found the rounded contour of her bare breast under her blouse she shuddered convulsively against him, pressing her body forward, her breath coming and going quickly as he rubbed the raised bud of her nipple.

'Oh, yes,' she moaned, guiding his free hand to her other breast.

His tongue flicked against hers, exploring the softness of her mouth, while he massaged her breasts with his hands, rubbing the nipples with his thumbs until she wanted to collapse with the exquisite pleasure shooting through her.

The fumbling efforts of her boyfriends in the past faded in comparison to the expertise of his arousal.

It took a few seconds before she realised that he had pulled himself away from her. Even then, still feverish with desire, she thought nothing of it, stepping forward slightly to kiss him on his neck. It was only when he drew her back by her arms that she opened her eyes wide and stared at him.

'That,' he rasped, 'was a mistake.'

He released one arm to run his fingers through his hair, his face tight and expressionless.

Sanity was very quickly returning to her, and it wasn't a pleasant sensation.

Her brief confusion at his sudden rejection of her had evaporated; now she could see things very clearly indeed, and the hot flush of embarrassment washed over her.

'You're right,' she agreed stiffly, 'it must have been the wine and the moonlight.'

Wine and moonlight. What a joke, she thought bitterly. She would have reacted in exactly the same way if she had been stone-cold sober and standing in a bare room under a fluorescent light. She was painfully aware of her body still throbbing where he had touched her, and she clasped her arms across her breasts tightly.

What on earth had she been thinking of?

She looked at the rigid contours of his face and wanted to run, but her feet felt like lead weights.

'I've always made a point of avoiding married women, and engaged women fall into the same category.' He sounded angry with himself. 'Apart from which, you're a child. You barely know what you feel.'

'There's no need to make excuses,' she said harshly, 'we both agree that it was a mistake. But, just for the record, I'm not a child.'

He looked at her at that, his eyes almost silvery in the semi-darkness. 'Alyssia,' he bit out, 'I'm not interested in affairs. Now I don't know if you've been brought up on a diet of men who jump in and out of bed with whatever women take their fancy, but if you have then I suggest you go find one of them to satiate your appetite. You've obviously got problems with this engagement of yours, but don't come looking for answers in my bed.'

'That wasn't my intention!'

'Good,' he said coldly, 'just so long as we understand each other. I'm not blaming you for what happened, but——'

'Fine.' She hardly recognised her own voice. 'Then let's just leave it at that, and clear away these dishes.'

'Go upstairs,' he ordered harshly, his hands in his pockets. 'I'll get rid of these things.'

Alyssia gazed at him for a fraction of a second, then she took his advice and walked back to the house, when what she wanted to do was run as far away as she could from it.

He was right, of course; it had been a mistake, and one which she had no intention of repeating.

CHAPTER FOUR

ALYSSIA lay perfectly still under the warmth of the sun's rays, enjoying the way the heat wrapped itself around her so that she didn't feel like moving. She could hear the soft lapping of the sea, the rustling of the leaves in the trees, and she thought, If I can make myself totally relax then I'll be able to forget everything.

But, of course, that just wasn't possible. Her disappointment over Jonathan, which had driven her to France in the first place, had been relegated somewhere to the back of her mind. Now, in retrospect, she could see that marriage to him would have been a ghastly mistake, and that her reaction to discovering that he had been seeing other women while he had been engaged to her had had far more to do with wounded pride than with a wounded heart. And wounded pride was something that she could quite easily cope with when it came to Jonathan Whalley.

What she was feeling now, however, was biting into her with relentless ferocity. She might close her eyes but she couldn't blot out what had happened the night before.

She had made a complete fool of herself and had successfully lived down to every low opinion that Piers harboured about her.

She groaned and turned on to her side, propping her head up with her elbow.

Hadn't he already said that he disliked women who threw themselves at him? And wasn't that precisely what she had done? Sure, he had responded to her, but she knew that he would not have if she had shown the slightest sign of reluctance.

She replayed in her mind every detail of the night before, every provocative movement that had unconsciously invited him to make love to her.

Just as well that she had been at least spared the ordeal of having to face him this morning. The more time she had to lick her wounds, the better.

She thought back with bitter awareness of what the astrologer had told her when she had read her charts. That she was inclined to be impulsive, that the hurt of yesterday was easily forgotten under the blinding optimism that tomorrow would bring the fulfilment of her dreams.

At the time she had laughed at the observation, but wasn't that what she was doing now? Sweeping the debris of her engagement to some distant corner of her mind, and throwing herself trustingly at a man who, in the cold light of reality, had no time for her?

She turned over on to her stomach and tried to put things into perspective.

Piers Morrison was a dangerous stranger, one who made no effort to treat her with respect, far less subservience, and who had kissed her on the spur of the moment, then instantly regretted it because he basically didn't like her.

Of course, more fool her for having succumbed to the moment, but it was over and done with, and that was the end of it.

Put like that, it seemed a simple enough equation, and at least now, she thought, she could be on her guard, would not let anything get in the way of level-headed logic.

She wasn't aware of Piers approaching until he cast

a shadow over her, and she sat up, this time not bothering to wrap her beach-robe around her. She didn't give one jot about him, kiss or no kiss, and she was going to make that perfectly plain by ensuring that she didn't react to him at all.

'You're blocking out my sun,' she muttered, annoyed to feel her body tensing at his presence.

'Am I?' He stretched his towel alongside hers, and said derisively, 'I had no idea that it belonged to you.'

'What are you doing here, anyway?'

'Actually,' he said slowly, 'I came down here to talk to you about last night.'

There was a heavy silence and Alyssia could feel her heart thumping heavily in her chest. Her mouth felt dry, and it was an effort to reply.

'I thought we'd covered all that. As far as I can see, there really isn't anything else to talk about, is there?'

Piers didn't answer. He was lying prone, his eyes shut, clad in that pair of briefs that made her eyes linger far too long on his bronzed legs and flat chest.

'Well, is there?' she persisted, her voice flat.

'You don't love this boyfriend of yours, do you?' he asked shortly, turning to face her.

'What business is that of yours?'

'Just answer the question.'

'I won't do anything of the sort!' Her face was flaming red and her eyes sparkled darkly into his.

'Then I'll answer it myself. You don't love him, you probably never did. And I can tell that from the way you responded to me last night. If I hadn't stopped you would have made love with me, and that isn't the action of a woman desperately in love with another man, is it?'

'I don't have to answer that.' She picked up her book and began reading, making a show of turning the pages so that he was left in no doubt that his presence next to her was the last thing she needed.

Without saying a word, Piers took the book away from her and tossed it aside, then he held her face between his hands, so that she was forced to stare into his eyes.

'I'm talking to you,' he said through gritted teeth. 'Does your boyfriend know that, underneath that cool, butter-won't-melt-in-your-mouth exterior, you're a wildcat? My guess is that he doesn't.'

'No, he doesn't,' Alyssia said in a high voice, 'because I'm not when I'm with him!'

'You don't love him,' he ground out. 'Face it, if I were to kiss you now I would feel you come to life under my fingers. Isn't that true?'

'No! And what business is it of yours how I feel about Jonathan?'

'Plenty. Your father asked me to try and talk you out of this engagement, to try and find out what you felt about this boy. Now I have, and I'm telling you that if you marry him then you'll be committing the biggest mistake in your brief little life.'

His words rang in the clear air and she could feel her head swimming from the enormity of what he had just said.

'My father. . .?'

'Dammit!' He rubbed his eyes and sat up, releasing her. 'I shouldn't have said that.'

'My father asked you to try and talk me out of getting married?' Alyssia asked hollowly. 'How could he?'

'He was worried about you. Though, just for the record, I wouldn't have tried to do anything of the sort if it weren't patently clear that you don't feel anything lasting for your fiancé.'

'I don't want to listen to any more of this!' She stood up, her eyes burning, and began walking steadily towards the water, but before she could get there she felt his hand in her hair and he pulled her to face him.

'And was it part of my father's plan that you make love to me to convince me that marriage to Jonathan was the wrong thing?' she said angrily.

'You know it wasn't,' he said roughly. 'I'm not afraid to admit that I wanted you last night, more than I've wanted any woman for a long time.'

His eyes had darkened and he was breathing heavily.

'And is that supposed to make me feel better?' Alyssia shouted, humiliated.

'Dammit, woman,' he muttered, 'from what your father told me, Jonathan's a rich playboy. You would have eaten him alive.'

Alyssia stared at him, speechless for a moment.

'That's not true!'

'Isn't it? Why don't you stop ranting and raving for a minute and start being honest with yourself?'

'The way you were honest with me?' she asked acidly. 'You didn't feel a thing for me when you kissed me, did you? You only wanted to test your theory that I wasn't in love with my fiancé. You only wanted. . .'

Her mind was struggling to verbalise the emotions running riot inside her, but before she could complete the sentence she felt his lips on hers, hard and demanding.

With a massive effort she tried to fight him off, but he had locked his hands behind her neck, and all her efforts to squirm out of his grasp were useless.

But she wasn't obliged to return his kiss, and she didn't, keeping her mouth firmly shut, her body rigid in her attempts not to respond to him.

But, inside her, everything was melting. She closed

her eyes and, with a little groan of defeat, parted her lips to accommodate the onslaught of his probing tongue.

God, she wanted him. She hated him and she hated what he was capable of doing to her, but her hate wasn't enough to stop herself from feeling the forbidden pleasure of his hands on her body.

He was kissing her hungrily, then he lifted her off her feet and carried her to the water's edge, resting her on the sand so that their bodies could feel the gentle ebb and fall of the sea against them.

'No,' she said weakly. There was a whole fury of protestations hovering on the edge of her lips, but somehow she couldn't seem to find the energy to voice them.

His mouth, trailing wetly across her neck, nipping the soft flesh occasionally with his teeth, was having a drugging effect on her mind.

With one swift, violent movement he tore off her bikini top, exposing her breasts to his gaze.

'God, you're beautiful,' he muttered fiercely, holding one breast in his hands and raising it to his mouth. His tongue flicked out to caress her nipple, which was throbbing painfully, and with one anguished movement she pressed his mouth further down so that he was sucking on the rosy tip.

He disposed of the remaining barriers between them, and even the cold water lapping against their naked bodies couldn't cool her heated skin.

There would be a price to pay for this abandonment. She knew that, even as she knew that, whatever price had to be paid, she would rather pay it than deny herself the overwhelming need coursing through her.

His hands followed the contours of her body, tracing

a path along her thighs, parting them so that he could explore the moistness inside her with his fingers.

She moaned shakily, the water washing her hair around her face like a golden fan.

She closed her eyes as he thrust into her, moving with rhythmic deliberation until everything exploded in her, and she released her breath in one long sigh of physical fulfilment.

For the first time in her life she felt radiantly satisfied, as though she had somehow managed to find all the answers to every question she had ever asked about herself.

Then he slid off her and they remained lying next to each other, his arm still under her neck.

More than anything else in the world she wanted him to touch her again, but already some of the unadulterated pleasure was slipping away and the doubts were beginning to reassert themselves.

If he had regretted his kiss the evening before, how on earth was he going to view what had just happened between them?

And, after everything he had told her, how could she ever hope to salvage any of her dignity?

The desire to make love to him had been irresistible, but that temporary blindness had gone, and what she saw made her shudder.

She waited for him to be the first to speak, determined to take her lead from him.

'What happens now?' she finally asked when the silence between them had become stretched to breaking-point.

'Well, we certainly can't undo what's just taken place between us, can we?'

'Would you want to?'

He stared down at her, his eyes slate-grey.

'Things got out of control,' he said slowly. 'I knew they would, the minute I began kissing you, but I just couldn't help myself.'

'Nor could I!' She smiled timidly, but his expression was remote.

'Now do you believe me when I say that I didn't touch you in order to prove some theory about your boyfriend meaning nothing to you?'

'I believe you.' She wanted to cuddle against him, to feel his body warm and aroused against hers once again, but instinct told her that things could not be as simple as that. 'I had planned to break off my engagement with Jonathan anyway,' she said in a low voice. 'I had discovered a few things about him that were very . . .hurtful. I had also discovered that I had never really loved him.'

In fact, she thought, she had never even remotely known what love was because it was what she felt now, and it certainly was nothing like what she had ever felt before.

The hard set of his face precluded any such confession, however.

'Why did you get engaged to him in the first place?' he questioned softly.

Alyssia shrugged. 'We enjoyed each other's company, and I guess I felt safe with him, safe, at least, that he wasn't after my money, which is always a problem when you've got a very wealthy father.'

His lips twisted and she waited for the inevitable cynical response, but surprisingly it didn't come.

'Well, at least you're honest.'

She reached out to touch him and felt his body tense.

'I think there are a few things we ought to get straight,' he said coolly. 'We might have made love, but that's as far as it goes. A physical act. There's no point deliberating on whether it should have happened or not. The fact is, it did. But I've said this before, and I'll say it again. Emotionally you're a child, even though you have the body of a very desirable woman, and I have no intention of becoming involved with you. I wanted you then, and I still do, but that's as far as it goes. I don't want you to get any ideas about replacing Jonathan with me, because it just won't work. I've had my bite at love and I don't intend to taste that bitter fruit again.'

Alyssia sat up and stared across towards the horizon.

'You don't believe in mincing words, do you?' she asked in a brittle voice.

'I just don't want you to be hurt by me.'

'How considerate of you,' she responded with a choked laugh, 'it's so reassuring to know that you have my welfare at heart. And tell me, do you give that little speech to all the women you make love with?'

'For God's sake, woman!'

He sat up alongside her, but she refused to look at him, refused to let him witness the wet film over her eyes.

'You needn't worry; when I leave here you need never see me again, so that should set your conscience at rest.'

'I'm not saying that we pretend it never happened. I can't do that any more than you can. I'm simply saying that. . .' He paused, as if searching for the right words.

'That we're physically attracted to each other, and that's as far as it goes?'

'If you want to put it like that, yes.'

'Well, I hate to damage your enormous ego, but the last thing I want or need right now is any sort of involvement, as you put it, with a man. Any man!'

That, at least, she meant. She didn't want involvement with any man; it was simply a cruel twist of fate that she had got it, and there was no way that she was going to expose her vulnerability to him. Especially when he had made it crystal-clear where he stood with her.

She wondered what experience had moulded him into the cynical man that he now was.

A pointless exercise, she acknowledged to herself.

'I think you should know, though,' she added with a perverse sense of enjoyment, 'that I don't want to romp in the hay with you for the rest of my holiday here. I was feeling low and I gave in to a mad impulse.' She forced what she hoped sounded like controlled, nonchalant laughter. 'It's just the way I am, I guess.' Another attempt at laughter, which sounded slightly less controlled and nonchalant. 'I sometimes do things without thinking first. I didn't really give much thought to coming to France, and I certainly didn't give much thought to making love with you. If I'd known that I would have been given a long lecture at the end of the day, well. . .'

She allowed her voice to trail off, basically because she knew that if she didn't she would end up bursting into tears.'

'You wouldn't have done it.'

'That's right,' she confirmed brightly.

He looked at her through narrowed eyes, then he stood up.

'Well, now that we've both indulged in our little speeches, I think I'll head back to the house.'

She watched him as he walked away, unhurriedly, moving with the easy grace of some wild animal.

When he had vanished from sight she expelled a long sigh and allowed the mask to slip away from her face, slowing returning to her towel and lying down flat on it.

She picked up her book, looked at it sightlessly, and then stuck it over her face. She had no intention of returning to the house in a hurry. She would stay out here until evening, if it killed her in the process. She would rather die of starvation, or sunburn, than face Piers Morrison, who had revealed a side to her which she had never even suspected existed.

He had undermined all her carefully built-up controls, got under her skin in the most insidious way possible, and turned her from a cool little lady into a screaming fishwife.

Her friends back in London would never have recognised her as the Alyssia Stanley who had dozens of men trailing behind her, and who toyed with them but only for as long as it suited her.

And Jonathan would never have recognised her as the girl to whom he had become engaged, the easygoing girl whose only concern had been to have a good time, however much money it took.

How ironic that she felt so alive in Piers's company, the one man who could shrug her off as carelessly as he would shrug off a few flecks of sand from his T-shirt.

He was attracted to her, but basically, if he never touched her again, then it would be no great loss.

But, for her, it was another story. It was as though she had spent the past twenty-two years imprisoned in a shell, and had now broken free of it, and was tasting sensations which she had never dreamed possible.

It was nearly five o'clock by the time she made it back up to the house, which was thankfully empty. No sound of hammering anywhere, and no Piers Morrison to set her nerves on edge.

She found herself peering into nooks and crannies, not that he could manage to conceal himself into one, with his breadth, and was almost disappointed when she realised that he had most probably gone out.

She indulged in a blissfully long bath, taking time to wash her hair and then comb it out, before drying it with a hand drier.

Then she dressed carefully, slipping on a pair of cream culottes and a rose-pink silk blouse, one of her acquisitions from Nice.

Her tan was coming along nicely, she thought, which she had expected. She tanned easily, despite her fair hair, and she had spent long enough in the sun, trying to avoid the house.

She slipped on some flat sandals, and made her way downstairs to the sound of voices.

One of them female and distinctly familiar. She walked into the sitting-room, and there was Simone, a glass of wine in her hand, her face a picture of absorption as she listened to whatever Piers was telling her.

For an instant Alyssia felt a rush of jealousy, which she just as quickly stamped on. They had both turned as she had entered, and she had the stupid urge to tell them to carry on, she hoped she wasn't interrupting anything.

'Simone,' she said instead, 'what a nice surprise. What are you doing here?'

Simone flushed and said quickly, 'I thought I'd drop by to visit. It isn't every day that you decide to come to France.' She laughed and continued, 'Piers has been keeping me entertained while I waited for you. He's been telling me all sorts of stories about the places he's worked in.'

She sat on the sofa alongside Simone, shaking her

head to an offer of some wine and avoiding the temptation to look at him.

'Sure?' Piers asked. 'It's a particularly nice one.'

'I'll stick to mineral water,' Alyssia said, sourly noticing that Mr Charm was back on the scene when he continued his conversation with Simone as though she hadn't arrived on the scene at all. And Simone was responding to him with laughter and appreciation.

Alyssia watched from the sidelines, feeling like a fish out of water, watching Piers from under her lashes. He was not wearing his faded jeans, but a pair of creamy-coloured trousers and a short-sleeved shirt, and he had combed his hair away from his face. She thought uncharitably that he looked like a gangster, although there was nothing menacing in the smile that played on his lips whenever he addressed Simone.

'André's looking forward to seeing you next week,' Simone interrupted her thoughts, trying to include her in the conversation. It made Alyssia feel like a charity case. She could remember the times when she had patronisingly tried to include some wallflower into a party, inwardly breathing a sigh of relief that she wasn't like *that*.

'Is he?' Alyssia asked politely, unable to ignore Piers sitting to her left, one leg crossed over the other, his eyes looking at her narrowly.

'He wanted me to ask you where you'd like to go. I think he favours an intimate setting, but,' and Simone laughed, 'I told him that engaged women only favour intimate settings when it's with their fiancé. He was crushed at my logic.'

There was a brief silence, then Piers said, 'When is this lunch, anyway?'

Alyssia breathed a sigh of relief. She hadn't wanted to tell Simone about her decision to break off her engagement. Not yet. Jonathan deserved to know first. After she had talked with him she would let everyone else know.

'When are you meeting that brother of mine, Ali? Is it next Wednesday?'

Alyssia nodded, and Piers said smoothly, 'I could recommend a place, if you like.'

'Where?' Simone said enthusiastically. 'I'm always on the look-out for new restaurants. As you can probably tell from my figure,' and she looked at her plump legs with satisfaction, 'I like my food!'

Piers laughed warmly and Alyssia immeasurably less so. She recalled his words to her about needing to put on weight, and she looked at her friend, for the first time ever, with a sharp stab of jealousy, then she hurriedly wiped the expression from her face.

'It's a little place,' Piers was saying, 'quite hidden away from the public view, as a matter of fact. Specialises in seafood. They do a superb *loup de mer*. The patron is a personal friend of mine. Perhaps we could arrange to go as a foursome; we'd have no trouble getting a table if I make the arrangements.'

Simone's eyes were sparkling, and Alyssia said frigidly, 'I had no idea you were known in this part of the world.'

Piers shrugged. 'I've done a fair amount of work down here in the south of France, mostly on the Cap Ferrat. Don't forget I speak fluent French. Always a big help when you're working on the Continent.'

Simone gazed at him understandingly. 'Isn't it? André and I are both fluent, but I've seen how disadvantaged an outsider can be without any knowledge of the language.'

'Do you speak any languages?' Piers asked Alyssia pleasantly, and she again felt as though they were both making an enormous effort to include her in what they would have preferred to be an intimate tête-à-tête.

How could he be so polite when he had been fired by passion only a couple of hours before? But of course he was not inconvenienced by any feelings beyond passion, and wasn't lust something that could be quite easily forgotten?

'No,' she replied briefly, feeling more and more resentful.

Simone laughed, a bright tinkling laugh like bits of silver being jingled together. 'Oh, Alyssia never paid much attention to work, did you, Ali? She was always the brightest, and she was always the one who kept getting reports that she could do better. Do you remember we used to have a laugh about it?'

Piers looked at her with interest. Go on, she thought, let's all have a hearty guffaw at my expense. But he wasn't laughing. He was staring at her as though he was piecing together bits of her personality like a mathematician working on some equation.

Alyssia threw her friend a small smile.

'I'm sure Piers isn't at all interested in schoolgirl escapades,' she said pointedly.

'On the contrary.' He turned to Simone. 'Tell me more.'

Simone obliged, oblivious to Alyssia's meaningful glances. She didn't want her past discussed with him— he wasn't interested in it, for heaven's sake—but she realised that there was no way that her friend could possibly be aware of those undercurrents.

She knew that to outside eyes they were behaving like two civilised adults, even though that was the last thing she felt.

'Well, everyone envied her. She was the most beautiful girl in the entire school. And she always did whatever she wanted, which was mostly enjoy herself and ignore her homework. Except for art. You were good at art, weren't you, Ali?'

'Yes,' Alyssia managed to mutter. The picture Simone was painting was precisely what Piers would have expected. Alyssia Stanley, the dizzy blonde. She stood up abruptly. 'What are we going to do about eating tonight?' she asked, thinking that any conversation they could have would be better than the one they were having at the moment.

Simone sprang to her feet. 'I've brought some stuff with me!' she exclaimed, reaching over for her car keys. 'It's all in the car. Some pâté and Brie, and a couple of sticks of French bread. Never let it be said that I visit empty-handed!'

'Why didn't you pursue your art?' Piers asked her curiously, standing next to her as Simone rushed outside to fetch the bags of food.

You're not really interested, she thought ill-humouredly. She gave a cool little shrug and concentrated on the scenery outside the window.

'If you must know,' she said finally, not looking at him, 'I didn't much see the point.'

'You mean because you didn't have to get a job if you didn't want to?'

Another little shrug.

'You're not still dwelling on our conversation on the beach, are you?' he asked with a hint of impatience.

'Of course not,' Alyssia lied.

'Because we're adults,' he continued, as though she hadn't spoken. 'We made love, but life will carry on, and while we're under the same roof I think a verbal truce is in order.'

'Of course.' The words were stiff and she still kept her eyes averted. God, it hurt to think that their love-making meant so little to him that he could dismiss it with so little difficulty.

Simone rushed back into the house, dumping the bags on the kitchen table, calling out for someone to give her a hand.

'I think she means you,' Alyssia said to Piers. She hated how she sounded, but she couldn't seem to snap out of it.

Simone was busy unpacking the bags, finding her way around the kitchen, asking whether there was any garlic because she was pretty efficient at making garlic bread.

Piers walked off to help her, and Alyssia remained where she was, listening to their friendly banter, not quite knowing what to do with herself.

Eventually she strolled in to join them. Simone was wonderful in a kitchen. She had very nearly done a cordon bleu cookery course after she had left school, only deciding at the last minute to reinvest her time and money in the boutique instead. Right now the counter was laden with implements that Alyssia could barely recognise, far less use.

She shuffled around uncomfortably, finally deciding to cut the bread because it was the one thing she could at least guarantee not to spoil.

If she were her normal self she would be pottering happily around Simone, laughing whenever she got in her way and sticking her fingers in the food.

But, with Piers there, she watched instead as they worked together, Simone quickly preparing the garlic butter, and making the salad dressing as he chopped the lettuce.

They made a good pair, both dark-haired, Simone animated and bubbly, laughing as he related amusing anecdotes about his travels.

Alyssia had for some reason thought that he spent the majority of his life in England, but it turned out that, although he owned a flat in London, he spent quite a lot of time working overseas.

Was that how he had developed the deep tan that made him look somehow so vital?

They ate out in the garden, and, although the meal was a cold one, and quickly prepared, it tasted delicious. The bread was hot and crusty, and the pâté was superb.

'So what are we going to do about next Wednesday?' Simone asked as she was leaving.

Piers looked at Alyssia, and she shrugged, as though to imply that they could trek along if they liked, it really didn't bother her one way or another.

'I'll leave you two to sort it out,' he said as they walked back inside.

Simone linked her arm through Alyssia's, and smiled. 'A foursome would be nice,' she mused, 'and look at it this way, we can be your chaperons.'

Alyssia strolled out to the car with her friend, relieved that he had remained in the kitchen, and turned to her. 'I'm sorry if I've been a bit below par this evening,' she apologised.

Simone squeezed her arm sympathetically. 'I did wonder whether you didn't want me there,' she said.

'What? Just the opposite. The more people there are around, the less time I have to spend trying to be civil to Piers Morrison!'

'Really?' Simone said thoughtfully. She opened her car door, and tossed her handbag on to the passenger-seat. 'I have to be honest, Ali, I didn't exactly drive out here just to see you. Not,' she continued hurriedly, 'that I didn't want to. But I quite wanted to see Piers again. I like him.'

Alyssia felt her blood freeze. The response was instantaneous, then she was ashamed at her reaction. So Simone was attracted to Piers. So what? He was as free and as single as a bird, as he made sure to tell her, and they clearly got along well. They had spent the entire evening chatting like old friends, while she had preserved her silence on the sidelines.

'You're welcome to him,' she said quickly, adding for more credibility, 'although I have to say, there's no accounting for taste.'

Simone looked at her for a moment.

'Sounds great in theory,' she speculated, 'but I don't quite think it's the same in practice.'

'What do you mean?' Alyssia looked at her friend, puzzled.

'I mean,' Simone said gently, 'that I might find him very attractive, despite all your dark and desperate misgivings, but it's not mutual.'

'You seemed to be getting along well enough.'

'Oh, that's true. We were getting along well enough. Like a couple of chums, but that's about as far as it goes. I don't excite him.' She laughed ruefully, and Alyssia felt a treacherous stab of delight.

Simone looked at her for a while, then she said, 'Now, about next Wednesday. Shall we meet up as a foursome?'

And they agreed to. Why, Alyssia thought, she had not jumped at the idea the moment it was suggested was anybody's guess. It really was a very good plan, because it would save her the potential embarrassment of André getting amorous over the starters. Not that she couldn't handle him, but it was so much better if the situation did not arise in the first place.

She walked back into the house, and Piers glanced at her with one raised eyebrow.

'Feeling better?' he remarked.

'Better than what?' she asked innocently, thinking that two could play at that game of acting as though everything were the same as it had always been.

'Better than you did for the entire evening.'

'Yes.' She threw him a wide smile. 'I feel fine. If a little tired, so if it's all the same to you, I think I'll make a move to bed now.'

The cool grey eyes swept over her, until she could feel herself flushing under his gaze.

'Fine,' he said tersely. He took a step towards her and for one heart-stopping moment she thought that he was going to kiss her, and then where would she and her collection of high-minded resolutions be?

But he simply side-stepped her to pour himself a glass of wine.

'Don't worry,' he said softly. 'I'm not about to touch you.'

And, with his words ringing in her ears, she fled up the stairs, not relaxing until she was warmly cocooned in bed, with only her thoughts for company.

She had not drawn her curtains, and she turned on her side, staring out at the velvety darkness, listening to the little noises that came wafting through the open window.

I've changed, she thought, I'm not the same shallow little girl who first came here to lick her wounds before returning to her life of perpetual glamour and moneyed ease.

Now she had fallen in love with a man who infuriated her, and turned her on, and had managed to read her like a book.

Wouldn't it have been wonderful if her love had been returned.

And then she had the stirrings of an idea.

She closed her eyes and told herself that that was simply succumbing to a whim, but why not? She had consulted an astrologer once before, even if it had only been for a lark, so why not consult another one now? Why not see whether their opinions varied and whether, she thought distantly, her stars could tell her which way now to turn?

CHAPTER FIVE

ALYSSIA'S brilliant idea to consult an astrologer seemed slightly less than brilliant when she awoke the following morning.

For one thing, the clear weather had given way to a furious downpour of rain. Not the fine, lifeless drizzle that she was accustomed to in England, but a driving torrent, complete with angry black skies and sea foaming furiously against the rocks.

A day to remain indoors. But indoors meant her thoughts and Piers, neither of which she felt strong enough to endure, so she grimaced at the weather and resolutely plodded into the village, dripping over the telephone as she called the one and only astrologer listed in the directory.

This, she thought with a sheepish giggle to herself, was ridiculous. What could the stars tell her that she couldn't tell herself?

Nevertheless she found herself giving the details of her history to a woman over the telephone who fortunately spoke English, along, she was told, with five other languages. Was she the only one in this part of the world who only spoke one language? It seemed like it.

At least, she thought as the taxi carried her to the astrologer's home, she had not had the ordeal of having to explain her bizarre decision to go out to Piers.

She would not have told him where she was going, but for the life of her she would not have been able to invent a pressing enough reason for leaving the house, least of all with only the shelter of her flimsy summer hat, since an umbrella had not been top of her list of things to pack when she had hurriedly boarded the plane at Heathrow.

By the time the taxi driver pulled up outside the very normal house in the very normal street in one of the suburbs of Nice she had pretty much convinced herself that she was slowly going insane.

Consulting an astrologer on a Friday evening for a bit of a laugh with some of her friends was just about passable. Consulting one in a foreign country with no one but herself and her inner turmoil was, however, very uncharacteristic behaviour for her.

What next? she wondered. Magic potions and crystal balls?

She paid the taxi driver, stepped out of the car and surveyed the house sceptically, not caring that the rain was soaking into her.

By the time she decided that this really was a stupid idea the taxi driver had disappeared into the network of streets, and she had no choice but to gloomily knock on the front door and pray that it didn't mysteriously open of its own accord.

It didn't. A girl who looked barely older than herself opened it and smiled.

Alyssia smiled back and wondered whether she should pretend that she had somehow ended up at the wrong address.

'Miss Stanley?' the girl asked.

There went that little idea. Alyssia nodded and stepped inside out of the rain, allowing herself to be helped out of her jacket, and finding herself responding to the girl's general comments about the weather.

All the while she covertly glanced around her. Disarmingly normal. Much more so than the place she had visited in London, which had been dark and smelled of incense.

A simple little house, charmingly decorated in pastel shades and seeming very much to match its owner, who looked more like a housewife than she did an astrologer.

But it was still mad. She listened in silence while the girl, who insisted on being called Claire because, she explained, people viewed her profession with enough scepticism without her adding to it by adopting some theatrical and phoney title, informed her that she had managed to prepare her birth chart.

'Have you?' Alyssia tried not to sound like one of those sceptics, but how she wished that she had decided to go into Nice instead and do some shopping.

Who knows? She might well have been able to forget her problems in some of those delightful little boutiques. Whatever, she certainly wouldn't have been experiencing the gut-wrenching tension that she was feeling now.

'I have.' The girl grinned infectiously and Alyssia reluctantly smiled back. 'And there's no need to be so nervous. Believe me, I'm not a magician and I'm not about to cast some awful spell on you. In fact, astrology is only mysterious to people who don't know anything about it.'

'Actually, I have visited one. In London,' Alyssia confessed.

'So you more or less know what we're about.' Claire looked at her with a puzzled frown, which quickly cleared. 'I won't ask you why you've decided to consult another, but here's what I've deciphered about your birth chart.' Another of those engaging grins. 'We can compare notes with your first visit.'

And she sat down and proceeded to slowly tell Alyssia about herself.

And this time, without the distraction of her friends giggling in the background, she actually listened to what was being said, becoming absorbed in the detached examination of her character by a stranger.

Of course, she thought with a stab at realism, all this could apply to anyone. Even so, most of it was so pointedly on target that she began to leave some of her cynicism aside.

She heard words like 'impulsive', 'trusting', 'hot-tempered' being mentioned, and she slotted the adjectives into her own life, thinking back to all the things she had done in the past which conformed with the personality being dissected by the astrologer.

'You're forthright, strong,' Claire said, 'capable of great things, like most Aries women, but right now I sense that you're not particularly happy, and certainly there's some indication that a lot of your unique drive has been squandered away. You're born under the sign of Mars, a person born to rise to all sorts of challenges.'

Alyssia smiled. 'I feel very self-indulgent, listening to you talk about me.'

'Sometimes it helps. After all, how can anyone sort out their problems if they haven't come to grips with themselves?'

'So you can see that I have a few problems?' I can't believe I'm doing this, she thought, but it felt wonderfully liberating to be able to discuss her private thoughts with someone who had no involvement in her personal life.

She had never been able to talk about her fears with any of her friends. They would never have understood, would have perhaps backed away from the possibility of seeing anything but the smiling, assured, beautiful and wealthy Alyssia Stanley.

Claire nodded slowly. 'It's obvious, and it's nothing to do with your charts. It's obvious from the expression on your face, the way you're sitting. Lots of little pointers. In my trade you come to read people quite accurately before you've even glanced at a chart.'

'Must be useful.'

'It certainly is.' She gave Alyssia a searching look. 'I can't read your future, you know. Not in all its intricate details. But I can give you some idea of general trends in your life. Do you want me to do that? It's a sort of progression from the reading of the birth chart. The two are quite closely linked.'

Alyssia held her breath for what seemed like minutes.

Did she want to have her future read? Wasn't there something sinister about it all?

'There's no need to be afraid,' Claire said, reading her thoughts. 'I can't possibly tell you something like beware of crossing streets tomorrow because if you do there'll be an accident. As I said, I can only give you general hints.'

'Nostradamus,' Alyssia murmured.

Claire laughed. 'I'm surprised you've heard of him. Lots of people haven't.'

'I don't know. . .'

'Your problems centre around a man, don't they?'

Well, she thought resignedly, another chance to get out of this missed. Not, she admitted truthfully to herself, that she had really wanted to. She was curious, but it would be stupid to forget that curiosity had killed the cat.

'Well,' Claire carried on, filling in the silence, 'I can't tell you how old this man is, or precisely what he looks like, but I can tell you that he's managed to turn your world upside-down. And I'm pretty sure he's a Virgo.'

Alyssia started. Something in that statement harked back to what that other astrologer had said. Beware the Virgo threat.

She brushed the thought aside.

'I suspect that he's quite different from you, quite contained.'

Claire stood up and began walking around the room, idly picking up one of the many calculators lying around, her hand trailing over the volumes of books on the shelves.

'If things were going smoothly between the two of you then I doubt you would be here now, but they're not, are they?' She didn't give Alyssia time to respond. 'The fact is that you're treading a minefield, and minefields, if they're not manoeuvred through carefully, can prove very dangerous indeed.'

Alyssia's body was still and she was conscious of her breath coming and going quickly. She really didn't want to hear any more of this, but the astrologer's matter-of-fact tone of voice was deceptively hypnotic.

So she remained rooted to where she was, listening.

'This man of yours is very much a one-woman man.'

And I'm not that woman, Alyssia thought miserably.

'And,' Claire continued, confirming her misgivings, 'his heart is tied up with a woman, one who has been with him for many years now.'

'No!' The denial was spoken without thinking. She stood up quickly and began rummaging in her bag, desperately looking for some francs so that she could pay the woman and leave. She didn't want to remain here, to listen to all those things she had known already for herself.

'You're not going?' Claire asked, concerned.

Alyssia nodded, not trusting herself to speak.

'But there's so much more——'

'I really don't want to hear.' At last, her purse. She extracted the required amount of money and handed it to the girl. 'I have an appointment,' she apologised. 'I really can't stay a minute longer.'

'But——'

'You've been so helpful.' She paused, and said with genuine sincerity, 'It's been so good to talk about things, feelings.' She laughed unsteadily. 'Perhaps when I get back to London I'll invest in a pet, a dog, or maybe a cat, and then I can pour my heart out whenever I want to.'

'You really oughtn't to leave halfway through this session, you know. This man, yes, there's another woman in his life, but——'

'Thank you so much,' Alyssia interjected hurriedly, moving into the hallway.

The rain was still slating down outside.

'How will you get back?'

She shrugged. 'I'll make a dash for it.'

'Please stay,' Claire pleaded. 'Call a taxi. You can have a cup of tea while you wait. If you wish to hear no more then so be it, but you'll be dreadfully wet if you venture outside.'

It made sense, but right now she didn't feel at all sensible, and she didn't want to do anything sensible. She just wanted to dash out of the house and let the rain cool some of the thoughts flying around in her mind.

She only managed to hail a taxi after fifteen minutes of running, and when she did she was almost afraid that he would not drive her because of her soaked condition, but, after a stream of highly ominous muttering in French, he finally let her in.

'You soak my *voiture*,' he informed her, none too politely.

'Don't blame me,' Alyssia said disgruntedly, 'blame the rain.'

Right now the well-being of his car seat was the last thing on her mind.

Her thoughts were twirling around and, however much she told herself that all that astrology stuff was nonsense, she could not prevent the doubts that had taken root and now refused to be urged away.

It might all be nonsense, she thought, but it certainly tied a few things together. For instance, Piers's unforthcoming remark about avoiding love because he had once tasted it and it had left a bitter after-effect.

Why else would he have remained a bachelor? He was a handsome devil, clever and presumably extremely well off. The sort of man who could have his pick of women, so why hadn't he picked any?

If he was the sort who enjoyed playing the field then she might have understood, but he didn't strike her as being that type at all.

In fact, he had admitted as much.

No, however much she tried to dismiss what the astrologer had said, the words kept ringing in her ears until she thought she would scream.

He had made love to her because he desired her, and she had happily let him because she was in love with him.

The two feelings were poles apart.

This is ridiculous, she decided when the taxi finally pulled up outside the cottage, after what seemed like years of self-analysis. It was a stupid idea to waste an entire morning on a foolish whim, and it was even more stupid to believe it as though it were truth instead of conjecture.

'My money?'

The taxi driver's voice cut into her thoughts, and she managed an absent-minded smile.

'I have the living to make, you know.'

'Of course you do,' Alyssia replied, feeling slightly better now that she had succeeded in explaining away some of the astrologer's words. 'And here's some extra to get your car cleaned after I've dripped so much on to it.'

She handed him a wad of francs and was rewarded by a beaming smile.

'For the car, *non*?' He nodded to the back seat.

'*Oui.*'

There, she thought, she felt much better. And so, no doubt, did the taxi driver.

Maybe, she thought, she had been adopting entirely the wrong approach. She was in love with Piers, and, now that she had accepted the agony of knowing that her love wasn't returned, maybe she could fight for him, could fight to win his heart, because it was silly to assume that he had some sort of woman in his life simply because the astrologer, a girl hardly older than herself, had implied as much.

If there was another woman, where was she? He wasn't married, that was for sure.

She let herself quietly into the house, and immediately heard the sound of voices coming from the living-room.

Who on earth would venture out in weather like this? she asked herself. Apart, she thought drily, from complete nutcases like myself.

Precious few people knew where she was at this present moment in time and, besides, Simone had visited only the night before.

She removed her jacket and hung it over the hook

on the kitchen door, and did the same with her hat, then warily walked into the living-room.

They both looked up as she entered, but Piers was the first to speak.

'You look like a drowned rat,' he commented, raising one eyebrow. 'I wondered where you had got to.'

'The English,' the woman sitting next to him said, 'you are so crazy.'

Alyssia turned to face her, feeling all her carefully constructed optimism ebbing away.

She had an interesting rather than beautiful face, with sharp angles and large blue eyes, and a wide mouth that was smiling pleasantly in her direction. Like a lot of the French women, she was dressed to perfection, her straight dark hair coiled into an immaculate chignon at the back of her neck, her nail varnish perfectly matching her shade of lipstick.

Another woman. This was certainly another woman, and they were certainly sitting very close to each other.

'I'm sorry,' Alyssia said tightly, 'I didn't mean to intrude.' Some water dripped from the tip of her nose into her mouth and she wiped it away with one swift movement.

'You'd better get changed,' Piers said in an offhand voice, 'or you'll find yourself stuck in bed with pneumonia for the next month.'

'Piers, you are not going to make the introductions?'

Alyssia eyed the staircase with yearning. She really didn't want any introductions to be made.

'Of course. Nicole, this is Alyssia, the young girl I was telling you about. Alyssia, Nicole.'

Nicole gave her another warm smile and said in that charming broken English, 'The young girl must change, *non*? You seem as if you have been taking the walk in the rain. Silly, *non*?'

Alyssia stretched her mouth into a mimicry of a smile.

'Actually, I wasn't taking a walk. There are limits to my craziness.' I've been consulting an astrologer, she thought. At least that was under cover. 'Now, if you don't mind, I'd better go and change. I'll be down in a minute.'

'No rush.' Piers gave her a long, cool look and she turned away.

Of course there was no rush, she thought acidly, making her way up the stairs. He obviously had not expected her to return and, now that she had, she could damn well stay up in her bedroom until the cows came home, as far as he was concerned.

From behind her she could hear them resume their conversation in rapid French, punctuated by laughter. Were they touching one another? she wondered, and then thought bitchily that physical contact would have been hard to avoid, they were sitting so close to one another.

The thought was distasteful but it continued to play on her mind as she got dressed in a pair of jeans and a flowered silk shirt.

And they were still chatting comfortably with each other when she rejoined them in the living-room, feeling very much like a spare part.

'So you go shopping in this weather, *non*?' Nicole asked with a smile.

'*Non*,' Alyssia said, mastering the French word and deciding that it had a certain ring to it when used in conversation with this particular woman.

Not, she conceded grudgingly, that Nicole was dis-likeable. Just the opposite. She was charm itself. But there was no way she could bring herself to like the other woman, even though she suspected that, had the circumstances been different, she would have warmed to her immediately.

Then she pulled herself up. Why was she jumping to conclusions? If there was some raging love-affair between the two of them then there was no reason why it should be a cloak and dagger affair.

'Where exactly were you?' Piers asked, sitting back in the sofa, and clasping his hands behind his head.

'Out,' Alyssia said, with no attempt to elaborate, and gave a wide smile that encompassed the whole room.

'Ah,' Nicole nodded sympathetically, 'is sometimes better to keep the big spending to oneself, *non*? The men, they don't understand.' She looked warmly at Piers and he laughed softly under his breath.

Was she imagining it, or were his eyes gazing back at Nicole's like a lingering caress?

Any moment now, Alyssia thought sourly, and this scenario will turn into an X-rated movie.

She smiled frozenly as if to remind Nicole that she was a guest in *her* house.

'Oh, Alyssia isn't the sort to keep her spending a secret,' Piers mocked.

'No,' she agreed, with the same smile plastered to her face, 'I'm just your average free-spending, thought-less little rich girl.' She could have kicked herself for the remark, for allowing Piers to see how much he got underneath her skin, but she couldn't prevent herself.

Fortunately Nicole didn't understand a word of her answer, though, from the thunderous frown that crossed Piers's face, she would have been stupid not to have realised that Alyssia was being facetious.

Her grasp of English was obviously limited, and she was not much inclined to stretch it further.

She turned to Piers and resumed her intense conversation with him.

'It's rude to speak French when I can't understand what's going on,' Alyssia pointed out in a high, clear voice.

'It's rude to try and understand what's going on when it must be obvious that it's none of your business.'

Piers gave her a cursory glance, and the blood rushed to her hairline. Well, she felt in a fighting mood, and if he thought that he could make a fool of her in front of his girlfriend then he was in for a big surprise.

'I'd like to remind you that you're in my house,' Alyssia pointed out, with what she thought was unassailable logic.

'And therefore we should do whatever your ladyship says?'

'Something like that,' she responded with anger in her voice. She knew that she was making a spectacle of herself with her childish outburst, but she couldn't seem to help herself.

'If you'd rather we left, Alyssia, then just say so, instead of beating around the bush with that sharp little tongue of yours.' He gave her a hard, level look.

'I never said that,' she muttered.

He turned away from her impatiently, and began talking to Nicole, both of them gesticulating, their voices overlapping in their haste to finish what they were saying.

Alyssia looked at his expressive hands, the long, clever fingers, and she wondered how well he really knew this woman. Had he slept with her?

Her mind gnawed away at the questions. She tried to imagine them in bed together, and found that the thought made her feel physically ill. But, once she began thinking along those lines, she was horrified to find that she could not stop.

When they stood up she thought with ill-humoured relief that Nicole was about to step into her car and drive away, but Piers turned to her and said in a flat voice, 'I'll see you later. I'm going out for a while. Eat lunch without me.'

Alyssia looked coolly at Nicole. 'Nice to have met you,' she said, her expression tight.

'Of course,' Nicole said. 'I am sorry we not have longer time to know each other, but I am having to rush. I have the husband and the child waiting for lunch.'

The husband? The child? Good grief!

The door slammed behind them and she listened, rigid, as the car purred into life and accelerated away.

Then she sat down heavily on the sofa. It was as if all her energy had been sucked out of her.

The final pieces of the puzzle had now been slotted into place. Nicole was married. More than that, married with a child. Piers was in love with a married woman. That would explain so much. It did explain so much.

The astrologer had been right to warn her off, had been right that his heart was tied up elsewhere. How bitter must he be to find himself in the position in which he was now?

A million questions sprang to mind. How long had he known her? They had the easy familiarity of two people who knew each other very well indeed, and had done for a very long time. Had he been in love with her before she had married? Were they sleeping together now? She remembered what he had said about steering clear of married women, and she decided that they probably weren't, not that the thought gave her any pleasure.

God, how she hated this.

She dragged herself from the sofa and listlessly prepared herself some lunch, making do with bread and Camembert cheese and some of the pâté which had been left over from the night before. And she found herself unwillingly waiting for Piers to return, watching the door, listening for the sound of the car.

It was laughable, she thought. She had never been the sort of girl to hang around, waiting for a man. She had never had the need. All her life, from as far back as she could remember, she had been in demand. Men waited for her phone call, for her appearance at their doorstep, not the other way around.

So why was she sitting here now, moodily watching the rain pelting down outside the patio doors?

Of course, she knew quite clearly what she should do. She should leave, return to England, fly back to the security of the life she had always known. But, she thought defensively, that would be running away.

She seemed to have spent the past few years running away. From herself, from any sort of commitment to do something useful with her life, from her dilemma with Jonathan.

What was that the astrologer had said? That she was the sort of person who faced challenges head-on?

Well, this was the greatest challenge of her life and she would damn well face it if it killed her.

She would get through the next few days of being in the same house as Piers and then she would leave, and she would somehow get through the rest of her life without him.

She picked up a piece of paper and began drawing little cameo pictures of the bowl of fruit on the sideboard, of the flowers in the garden, bending under the wind.

Maybe she would take up her art again, and when she had polished that rusty talent perhaps volunteer to teach handicapped children.

Her heart wasn't in what she was doing, though. And her mind certainly wasn't. Her mind was miles away, focused on imaginary scenarios being played out between Piers and Nicole. Where were they now? Maybe he was helping her prepare the meal for the husband and the child, stifling the urge to take her in his arms. Or maybe she was wildly wrong about both of them. Maybe they were in some room somewhere where the husband and the child were not on either of their minds.

The scrap of paper was furiously filling up with pictures of trees and flowers, which Alyssia hardly looked at at all.

He should be working, she thought, her mind taking off down another route. Wasn't he supposed to be doing all this as a favour to her father? Did he think he was so important that he could finish the cottage in his own sweet time? A spot of work here and there, liberally interspersed with rendezvous with an old flame?

She would mention that to him when he decided to make his reappearance.

Then she changed her mind. She wouldn't. He would jump to all the wrong conclusions. For starters, he might get it into his head that she was jealous.

I'm not jealous, she told herself, not really. This awful pain eating away at me is simply anger at myself for the stupid situation I'm in now.

The next time she consulted her watch she saw with surprise that it was nearly six o'clock.

The storm outside was beginning to abate, but the sky was still ominously overcast and the wind was paying havoc with the trees.

She was so absorbed in her thoughts that she didn't hear the taxi pull up outside at all, nor the opening and closing of the kitchen door.

She just heard footsteps behind her, looked around, and there he was, standing behind her for all the world as though nothing between them had changed.

'What are you doing?' he asked conversationally, divesting himself of his jacket and slinging it over the sofa.

'Nothing.' She crumpled the sheets of paper and tossed them on the coffee-table.

He was standing behind her now, and she could feel the energy emanating from him like a tangible force.

Before she could follow his movements he was by the coffee-table, the long fingers carefully flattening out the creased pieces of paper she had derisively hurled there.

'Alyssia Stanley, the artist,' he said in a speculative voice. 'They're very good. Very fresh.'

'You don't have to patronise me!'

The moment the words left her lips she regretted them. This wouldn't do at all. She would have to control that urge to speak without thinking, would have at least to look cool and controlled, even if that was not how she felt.

He eyed her over the sheet of paper. 'Is that what I was doing?'

'Isn't it? It's what you always seem to be doing.' She had spoken so softly that she was surprised that he had even heard her.

But he had. The grey eyes flicked over the curves of her body, and finally rested on her face. 'I don't know,' he said smoothly, 'I can think of a couple of occasions when patronising you was the last thing on my mind.'

Alyssia felt the colour rush to her cheeks.

'I don't know what you mean,' she mumbled.

'Don't you?' He sat down next to her and the sofa dipped under his weight so that it was an effort to keep her body erect.

'I. . .' she said in a rush, 'you. . . I didn't think that you knew a great deal about art.'

He smiled and she knew that he was quite aware of how addled she was, and why. How gauche and transparent she must seem. The thought made her anger flare up again.

'Of course I do,' he replied, relaxing and stretching his long legs out in front of him, so that they were within a hair's breadth of brushing against hers. 'In my profession, it pays to have an eye for art. Besides,' he shrugged, 'I collect paintings. It's my hobby.'

'Expensive hobby,' Alyssia commented, her body taut.

'It can be,' he agreed, 'which brings me back to your pictures. They're good, very good. Is that where you were this morning? Buying art supplies?'

Alyssia nodded quickly. Art supplies? The only brush she possessed was the one she used for her make-up, and the only pencil the one she had found lying about on the sideboard.

'You should have told me, I would have come with you, offered some advice.'

'And missed Nicole's visit?' she couldn't prevent herself from asking any more than she could prevent the edge that had entered her voice. 'She's very nice,' she continued in a more neutral tone. 'Does she live around here?' She picked up one of the crumpled scraps of paper and began staring fixedly at the pictures on it.

'As a matter of fact, she does,' Piers said briefly.

'How long have you known her?'

'Why the questions?'

Alyssia turned to face him, her eyes round and innocent. 'No reason,' she said, 'just the same polite curiosity that made you ask all those questions about Simone and André. You needn't answer if you don't want to.'

'You're not telling me anything I don't already know. Believe me, when I don't want you prying into my life you'll be the first to know about it. But, since you're so interested, I've known Nicole for a long time.'

Then why aren't you married to her? Alyssia wanted to ask.

He stroked a strand of hair away from her face, and her body froze.

'Would you like some coffee?' she found herself blabbing.

'Not coffee, no.' He smiled, a slow, charming smile that made her blood turn to water.

He wants me, she thought with panic, and then hot on the heels of that thought came another; he wants me because he's spent the afternoon and evening with the woman he loves but can't have, and so he wants to release some of that frustration on me.

She jerked back convulsively.

Her heart was beating wildly now. Any minute, she thought, and it'll be in my mouth.

She could feel her breasts hard under the thin cotton of her blouse, the nipples pushing against the material, yearning for the feel of his hand. But there was no way she would allow herself to be carried away by that hypnotic pull that he had over her.

Not when she knew that he really wanted someone else.

'You're not really seeing me, are you?' she accused harshly.

'What are you talking about?' Piers asked, his voice razor-sharp.

'You know what I'm talking about.' She thought about what the astrologer had said and decided to take a gamble. She *had* to find out whether her suspicions were true or not, and how else could she ever hope to do that if she did not ask him directly?

He sure as hell was not going to volunteer the information.

She knew that he was not going to like her question, might well accuse her of all sorts of things, not least acting like a jealous wife instead of a woman on whom he had clapped eyes only a matter of a few days before. But she would risk his anger to satisfy her need to know.

'No, I damn well don't know what the hell is going on in that pretty little head of yours, but I'm fast losing patience. If you have something to say then say it, but stop beating about the bush.'

Alyssia took a deep breath to steady her nerves, and then said unsteadily, 'Nicole is more to you than just a friend, isn't she? You're more involved with her than you want to let on, aren't you?'

'What business is that of yours?' he grated.

'We made love!'

'And that gives you some sort of hold over me?' He laughed derisively. 'I had no idea that you were the sort to put a great deal of store on the value of one-to-one relationships.'

'You still haven't answered my question.'

'All right, then, I'll answer your question. Yes,

Nicole and I go back a long way, and yes, you could say that we're involved on more than just a superficial level. Now is your curiosity satisfied?'

Alyssia's mouth dropped open and her eyes widened.

Well, she had wanted answers to her questions, hadn't she? Now she had got them she just wanted the earth to open up and swallow her.

'You met her here, didn't you?' she whispered with a stab of insight. 'I mean, right here, in this village.'

'Yes,' Piers bit out, 'I met here right here in this village.'

'That's why you took this job, free of charge.'

He shrugged. 'One of the reasons.'

'I see.'

Night had descended quite suddenly, and, as neither of them had bothered to switch on any lights, the house was in complete darkness, a darkness made all the heavier by the remnants of the storm outside.

'I think I'll go to bed now,' she said in a small voice.

He stood up abruptly and she followed him with her eyes, aching at the sight of his powerful body.

'Alyssia,' he began, 'there are things that you don't understand. You're a child, dammit, and——'

'I understand,' she responded coldly, 'a lot more than you give me credit for. But, as you said once, we're two adults and I have several more days here. In a way, it's a good thing that the air's been cleared.' She laughed brightly. 'It's always better knowing where one stands, don't you agree?'

'And where do you stand?' he asked softly.

He was facing her, and the half-shadows lent his body a forbidding, dangerous air that seemed to engulf her.

'I don't like sharing my men,' she said, intending to

sound far more experienced than she was and succeeding. 'You were an interlude.'

'An interlude.' She couldn't make out the expression on his face as he spoke, and in a way she was glad that she couldn't. 'Well,' he said grimly, 'it's probably better that way. The last thing I would have wanted was for you to become emotionally involved with me.'

There was a silence that seemed to last to eternity, then her pride brought her to her feet and filled her cheeks with hot, angry colour.

'How dare you even suggest that I am?' she hissed. 'How dare you?'

'I'm not suggesting that you are. I'm suggesting that you avoid it.'

He stared right into her eyes, and she thought that she had never been so enraged in all her life. All the anger she had ever felt seemed to shrink into no more than fits of petty temper in the face of what she was feeling now.

White-hot rage that was all the more potent because it originated from humiliation, and from the sickening knowledge not only that she was infatuated with him, but also that he had recognised the fact.

'Thank you so much for the advice,' she told him with icy calm, 'but I can assure you that it wasn't necessary.'

He nodded, looked as though he was going to say something else, but then thought better of it, and headed off upstairs, leaving Alyssia clutching a confusing array of emotions, none of which she felt she could deal with.

She wanted to drop off the face of the earth, then she wanted him to drop off the face of the earth, but, since neither was a possibility, all she wanted to do was to retreat to the darkest corner of the house, and lick her wounds.

If only she could turn back the clock she would never have come to this wretched country in the first place. If she had stayed in England everything would have been all right.

She listened to the silence around her, and then tiptoed up to her bedroom, ignoring the hungry rumblings of her stomach.

It was only when she was in bed that the hot tears poured down her cheeks. At least one thing had been achieved, at least now she knew the truth about where she stood. Wasn't that something to be grateful for?

CHAPTER SIX

ALYSSIA ended up looking forward to her lunch with André far more eagerly than she had originally thought possible. For one thing, it would be a chance for her to escape some of the tension in the house.

Not, she thought as she dressed unhurriedly on Wednesday, that Piers seemed in the least bothered by any tension. He seemed to have dismissed their disturbing conversation to some distant recess in his mind.

Oh, no. She was the one who felt the tension. Every time he addressed her she felt her body freeze, though she was getting much better at hiding her reactions.

In a month's time, she decided, applying some pale lipstick, I'll be laughing about all this. Wondering what on earth I'd ever seen in that. . .that—for a moment the description failed her—that ruthless, dangerous stranger.

There. Her make-up was all applied, and she surveyed her reflection with an objective eye. No eye make-up, just a touch of mascara, some blusher and some lipstick, and that glowing tan that so emphasised the fairness of her hair.

She slipped on a figure-hugging beige dress which showed off all the curves that still managed to exist in the right places, despite her total aversion to most forms of exercise, apart from dancing.

I'm lucky, she told her reflection, and in a few days' time I'll be far away from this place, and without Piers around I'll be able to put things back into perspective.

He yelled up the stairs for her to hurry up.

'We want to make it to the restaurant some time this century!' she heard him informing her.

In the privacy of her bedroom she grimaced in the direction of the voice and made her way downstairs, taking her time, not caring if he went grey in the process of waiting for her.

It annoyed her that, despite everything that had been said and done between them, and which obviously had meant absolutely nothing to him, since his attitude towards her was the same as it had ever been, she still found it difficult to control her emotions in his presence.

His dry sense of humour still had the capacity to make her lips twitch in amusement, even as she recognised that there was nothing remotely amusing about the way she felt about him.

'About time,' he told her, his eyes wandering the length of her and flicking back to her face.

'We wouldn't have to try and beat the clock,' she informed him, looking away, 'if that car of yours wasn't so slow. We'd almost do better cadging a lift off a couple of tortoises.'

The sharp contours of his face relaxed into a grin, and Alyssia frowned. She didn't like to see that grin. It reminded her too strongly for her own good that he had been doled out far too much fatal charm.

'I think it makes a refreshing change from my Jaguar back in England,' he murmured. The grey eyes flicked over her again, and she felt that familiar tensing of her body.

It would have been so much easier if he had remained hostile towards her, but she could sense that that simply would not have been in keeping with his personality. He would have seen it as infantile behaviour. Prolonged temper tantrums were not part of his personality.

Maybe that was one of the things that she found so endearing. The part of him that was so completely different from her own.

She looked at him, casually dressed in a pair of olive-coloured trousers and a pale tan T-shirt, and wondered how such ordinary clothes could assume such a ridiculous quality of distinction on him.

The journey into Nice seemed to take forever. The car spluttered and shuddered, and Piers apologised so glibly on its behalf that she was left in no doubt that he was laughing at her. But if he thought that he could goad a reaction out of her then he was sorely mistaken. She pretended not to notice the mocking drawl behind his words and instead concentrated on the scenery.

The sun had returned with vigour, giving the trees and leaves a crispness that almost hurt the eye. There was the faintest of breezes that took away some of the heat, making it beautifully cool.

'Are you going to tell them about your decision to break off the engagement?' he asked suddenly, interrupting her thoughts.

Alyssia looked at the unsmiling profile, the strong hands resting lightly on the steering-wheel, and wished that she had never allowed herself to confide in him.

He knew far too much about her for her liking.

'No,' she said abruptly. 'I'll tell them after I've told Jonathan.'

'That's fair.'

'Thanks, but I really don't need your opinions on the subject.'

He glanced across to her, then his eyes were back on the road. 'Why are you always on the defensive?' he asked. 'If you're not careful you'll start developing lines of discontent long before you're out of your youth.'

'Don't tell me that you trust the whole world,' Alyssia couldn't resist rejoining.

'No, of course not. I'd be a complete idiot if I thought that I could go through life and not bounce into the occasional person who didn't have my welfare at heart, and I'm no idiot. But that doesn't mean I have to work on the premise that everyone's untrustworthy until proven otherwise.'

'Except in love,' Alyssia said lightly.

'Haven't we beaten that subject to death already?' he asked, his voice hardening. 'Or maybe you'd prefer to be invigorated by another stalemate argument with me on the subject.'

Alyssia averted her eyes from him. She didn't want to be having this conversation. She didn't like being made to feel like an underage teenager who couldn't control her emotions.

In fact, she didn't want to be having *any* conversation with him. She stared out of the window and thought she could write a book in the time it was taking them to get to Nice, which really was just around the corner.

Was he driving slowly on purpose, or had the car decided of its own free will that it was a nice day to relax?

'If you want to take a detour from polite conversation then let me ask you this: despite all that money and all those fancy clothes and wild parties, you're not very happy, are you?'

Alyssia flushed. 'That's none of your business!'

'Not really, but I'm making it my business.'

'Why?' she asked. 'Because you still think of me as a child who needs your psychoanalysis?'

She was losing all sense of perspective. She knew

that. Their argument a few days ago was still hovering at the back of her mind, still had the power, in fact, to make her cringe with shame, and it lent an edge of petulance to all her answers to his questions.

'I wish I did,' he muttered under his breath.

'And I wish that we'd continue talking about impersonal things. I'm tired of arguing.'

She looked mutinously at the scenery and listened to the clunking noises of the car as it trundled along, allowing minimal ventilation through the tiny windows that only slid across to open halfway.

Piers didn't say anything, but he didn't press the point with her. Probably, she thought, because it didn't matter enough to him. If only there were a radio she would have turned it on, loudly, but, of course, no such luck. Since when did metal creepy-crawlies get kitted out with stereo systems? A radio would probably be worth more than the car itself. She looked at the dashboard, and thought suddenly that, after all her comments about the damned thing, she was becoming quite fond of it.

I must be losing my head, she thought. First I make the mistake of falling in love with this man who probably won't remember what I look like the minute I leave this place, even though he's not averse to the idea of making love to me while we're under the same roof.

Then I run off in a storm to see an astrologer. Now I find myelf liking this rustic way of life.

Simone and André would restore her sense of sanity.

They were waiting for them inside the restaurant, which turned out to be a smallish place that somehow managed to achieve an atmosphere of casualness and intimacy at the same time.

It had a cellar-like quality about it, with its abun-

dance of wine bottles everywhere, some of them looking quite ancient.

A place for lovers, Alyssia thought suddenly.

She dragged herself back to reality, and began
joining in the conversation, listening with amusement
while Simone regaled them with stories of some of
their customers—fat women with strange tastes in
colour, young girls with more money than sense.

'And, of course,' Alyssia said, laughing, 'you make
it your duty to point out to them when they're about to
make a horrendous error of judgement?'

'I do, actually,' Simone admitted. 'I couldn't live
with myself if I sent someone on their way with an
outfit that made them look awful.'

There was a lull in the conversation, and Simone
shot her brother a glance from under her lashes.

'What's up?' Alyssia asked curiously. She knew that
look from old, and it wasn't one that she particularly
liked. It usually preceded a sentence that started, 'I
know it's none of my business, but. . .'

She sipped from her glass of wine and impatiently
waited for Simone to speak.

'I'll tell you about it later,' Simone said, her face a
picture of embarrassment.

'Tell me what later?'

André was toying with the stem of his glass, and
Simone looked quickly at Piers and then looked away.

'It doesn't matter.'

There was another uncomfortable silence, and
Alyssia clicked her tongue impatiently.

'Just tell me what's on your mind, Simone,' she said
flatly,' and don't try to change the subject.'

'I'd rather not. Really. Not in front of Piers.'

Piers didn't look in the slightest bit put out by this
statement. He settled back in the chair, his leg acciden-

tally brushing against Alyssia's, and looked as though he was highly intrigued by the conversation and in no hurry to excuse himself.

'Never mind me,' he said smoothly, 'I'll just listen in silence. You won't even know I'm here.' He looked challengingly at Alyssia and she sighed in resignation. They had already shared their bodies; it seemed a little pointless to ask him to leave over something that Simone had to say.

'Go ahead, Simone,' she said wearily.

'Well, I wasn't going to say anything, but——'

'But I insisted,' André intervened.

'And?' Alyssia looked questioningly at them. She had a good idea of what this revelation was going to be, and was even beginning to enjoy their discomfiture.

'It's about Jonathan,' Simone began. She cleared her throat and glanced across to her brother for inspiration.

'You've heard rumours about him?' Alyssia prompted. 'Rumours that he's been fooling around behind my back?'

'You know?'

She nodded at her friend. 'That's why I came over to France. I needed to sort things out in my mind.'

She sneaked a glance at Piers, who still looked highly entertained at events.

'Of course,' Simone muttered, blushing, 'it might all be complete fabrication. It might. . .'

'It isn't.' Alyssia shook her head vehemently. 'I'm going to call the engagement off.'

For the first time Simone looked at Piers. 'You knew?' she asked, and he inclined his head to the affirmative.

Simone looked curiously at Alyssia, then back to Piers, as if trying to work something out.

'So you've succeeded, then?' she questioned. 'You've sorted it all out?'

'That,' Alyssia said pointedly, 'and a whole lot more besides.'

'Really?' Piers's voice from beside her was soft. 'What an enigmatic statement. Are you going to clarify it?'

'No,' Alyssia responded coolly, forgetting for a moment that she wasn't alone with him. 'But I'm sure you can work it out for yourself if you apply enough thought.'

'Excuse me,' Simone interrupted, 'but am I being dense? I don't quite understand. . .'

'It's nothing,' Alyssia mumbled, switching the conversation into safer waters, and allowing her thoughts to drift away.

It surprised her how little public knowledge of Jonathan's behaviour affected her. That had been one of the biggest worries when she had first fled to France: what was everyone going to say?

Now, she realised, she didn't much give a damn.

The whole business seemed to have shrunk in importance to the size of a peanut anyway. In fact, it had hardly crossed her mind at all for days now. If Simone had not mentioned his name she would completely have forgotten his existence.

She only realised that the meal had ended when Piers summoned across for the bill.

She had been totally engrossed in her thoughts, but her body must have switched on to autodrive because she had managed to eat the food on her plate without really tasting it, and had probably contributed to the conversation without even being aware of what she was saying.

The glare when they emerged from the restaurant was disorientating.

Simone kissed her warmly on her cheek, looked as though she was about to say something, and then thought better of it. André held her hand and squeezed it.

'I'll get in touch, if that's all right. Is it?'

Alyssia blinked at him. 'Sure,' she said vaguely.

'We can have some fun before you go.'

'Sure,' she repeated, parrot-like.

Fun? That implied being carefree, and she felt as though it had been decades since she had felt that way, and it had nothing whatsoever to do with Jonathan.

'You all right?' Piers asked when the two figures had melted away into the crowds.

Under the gruff tones she could feel his sympathy for her at being placed in such an awkward situation, and she made an effort to summon up some anger at his being sorry for her, but she couldn't.

'I've had more relaxing lunches,' she admitted ruefully.

'I don't think Simone would have mentioned it if she hadn't felt that it was for your own good,' he murmured. He had stuck his hands in his trouser pockets and was looking straight ahead, his eyes level.

'I suppose not,' Alyssia commented neutrally, then she said with a little more of her customary fire, 'although I feel as though I've gone through my entire life with people doing what they felt was best for me.'

'That's not so bad, is it?'

'Not bad, no, just a little irritating after a while.' She glanced across at him.

'Money does have its drawbacks, doesn't it?'

Their eyes locked together for an instant, and she

felt as though he was seeing right into her soul, into bits of her that no one had ever seen before.

'What do you mean?'

'I mean, you've been indulged for too long. You need taming.'

Alyssia blushed. He was right, of course, but his remark made her sound so *young*.

She doubted that he would ever have had reason to suggest that to Nicole. She seemed a woman with her head very levelly screwed on.

'What would you suggest?' she asked lightly. 'A diet of discipline and early nights?'

'I would suggest that you think a bit more carefully before you decide to commit yourelf to another long-term relationship.'

His statement pulled her back down to earth. Why did she let herself feel so safe with him, when to him she was nothing more than a hot-tempered child with a woman's body?

'Yes,' she replied tersely, 'I'll make sure that I draw up a balance sheet next time. Pros on one side and cons on the other.'

He shrugged. 'That could work. I think there's a lot to be said for arranged marriages, actually.'

'Are you always so unemotional?'

His eyes went a few degrees cooler. 'I've found that emotions can be a handicap. In fact, they can cause no end of problems.'

And being in love with a married woman certainly is a problem, she thought bitterly. 'So you steer clear of them now.'

'That's right,' he said shortly.

And so ends the discussion, she thought. However hard she tried to climb into his mind and find out what was going on in there, she never seemed to get beyond that barrier which he had laid down.

He let her see just as much as he wanted to reveal, and no more.

They walked the rest of the distance in silence, and by the time they got back to the car it was baking hot.

She could feel the plastic sticking to her tights as she sat down.

She lay back against the seat, her eyes closed, trying desperately not to react to his indifference.

It seemed that, every time she resolved not to let her wayward emotions get the better of her, he said something that had her responding to him like a fourteen-year-old star-struck teenager all over again.

She was hardly aware of the car pulling up outside the house, or of going up to her bedroom, claiming that she was too exhausted to relax on the beach and enjoy the remainder of the sunshine.

'Sure all this hasn't affected you more than you're letting on?' Piers asked, following her upstairs.

Alyssia spun around in panic. She didn't want him following her to the bedroom. He would fill it with his presence, and she didn't want that at all.

'Of course not!' she said more sharply than she had intended. 'You knew that I was going to break off the engagement anyway, so it's not exactly the end of the world for me. You don't have to feel sorry for me.'

Piers's grey eyes narrowed. He raked his fingers through his hair, as if debating what to say next, and she followed the movement.

Standing this close to Piers was enough to bring her out in goose-bumps, and she thought, I'll fight this desperate longing for him to the end.

'Whoever mentioned anything about that?'

'You don't have to. I can read it on your face. I just want to be alone, so if you don't mind. . .'

She looked pointedly at the stairs behind him, and he gave her a thorough scrutiny, as though trying to work out exactly what was on her mind.

'Do you know something?' he asked, thrusting his hands into his pockets and leaning indolently against the wall.

'What?' She licked her lips nervously and made every effort to appear casual.

'You're the most damned temperamental person I've ever come across in my life.'

She felt like screaming that she never used to be like that. That she had always been in control before he had come on to the scene and turned everything upside-down.

'I just want some time to myself,' she repeated calmly.

He shrugged and turned away. She heard him running lightly down the stairs, and breathed a long sigh of relief.

Jonathan had all but disappeared from her mind. She could cope with the Jonathans of this world. They were predictable. But she couldn't cope with Piers. He had managed to strip her of all her protective layers, and just being in the same room as him made her feel vulnerable and helpless.

She didn't want to feel that way. She couldn't afford to. No, she wouldn't allow herself to be rejected by him.

She went slowly into the bedroom and sat by the window, staring at the spectacular scenery outside, and not seeing it.

What was she going to do when she got back to

England? The mere thought of Piers no longer being around made her feel horribly empty and desolate.

She sat dry-eyed for what felt like hours, then she had a long bath and washed her hair.

She mentally steeled herself for the long evening ahead, but, as it turned out, it wasn't nearly as long as she had anticipated because towards the end of the evening she heard a sharp knocking on the door, and opened it to find André standing outside, a huge bunch of flowers in his arms.

She nearly fell on him in gratitude.

'It's only a bunch of flowers,' he said, pleased with her response, 'although I can guarantee that I have bought them, and haven't picked them on the way over. I thought they might cheer you up.'

'They have,' Alyssia told him, sniffing the delightful aroma of the blooms, 'more than I can say.' She waved him in to the sitting-room, and Piers looked up as they entered, his eyes expressionless as he took in the identity of the visitor.

'André,' he said in a flat voice, 'what are you doing here?'

Alyssia looked at Piers with a puzzled frown. She knew that he didn't much care for André, but he could at least have made a better attempt at disguising it.

André was undaunted by the lack of enthusiasm.

'I have come,' he announced with a sense of drama, 'to rescue the fair maiden from an evening of melancholy.'

Alyssia giggled, and Piers continud looking at their visitor, unamused.

'What a charitable gesture.' He moved across to them, and when he was standing next to André she noticed how much taller and more powerfully built he was. And, with that cool expression on his face, there was something daunting about him.

'Where's your sister?' Piers asked curiously. 'Shouldn't she be the one here instead of you?'

'I managed to talk her out of her mission of mercy,' André replied, grinning warmly at Alyssia. 'Besides, I'm much more accomplished at rescuing damsels in distress. A good meal at a good restaurant, and, hey presto, the beautiful lady will be back to her old, charming self.'

Alyssia was enjoying all this. André's flamboyance always had the capacity to make her laugh, and he was just what she needed.

She returned his warm grin with one of her own.

'What would I do without such knights in shining armour?' she asked lightly.

Piers looked at them with a frown.

'Much experience in trying to console women after broken engagements by making passes at them?' he asked.

There was a heavy silence.

Alyssia felt her temper begin to fray. Just who did Piers Morrison think he was?

'I think you're jumping the gun a bit here,' André volunteered awkwardly.

'Am I?' He turned to her. 'What would you say?'

'I'd say that you're being totally rude and arrogant,' Alyssia snapped, 'and I'd also say that I think a meal out with André will more than get me back to my old, charming self!'

André looked visibly placated.

'Shall we go?' He reached for her hand and kissed it with a flourish.

Piers leant against the door-frame and surveyed them in silence. She could well imagine what was going on in his mind: fickle, impulsive girl who flitted from one man to another without so much as a backward glance.

And she knew that she wasn't helping matters by playing the coquette with André, but suddenly she didn't care. It was all right for Piers: he had played with her for the hell of it, while making no bones about telling her that she was little more than a convenient body.

Well, if he thought she was a good-time girl then that was his affair.

'I'll see you when I see you,' she said, giving him a wide, plastic smile.

He had not budged, and if she hadn't known better she would have said that he was jealous, but, of course, the idea was ridiculous.

'Fine.'

'I'll make sure that I'll bring her back in one piece,' André was saying, but Piers had turned away and gave no indication of having heard what was being said to him.

He didn't glance in their direction as they left.

'What's up with him?' André asked, once they were outside and he had started the car.

Alyssia shrugged. 'Who knows? Male menopause?' she offered airily.

His reaction had bewildered her, but she didn't want to dwell on it, because she knew that she would inevitably end up spending the entire evening thinking of him, and then feeling frustrated and angry with herself for having given in to her private weakness.

No, she would enjoy this evening, she would let André entertain and amuse her, and she would not give in to useless introspection.

They drove out to a delightful restaurant, and Alyssia made a pig of herself. Starters, main course of *gigot d'agneau*, and a glutton's dessert of crème brûlée. They cracked open a bottle of wine, and by the end of the night she was feeling very pleasantly mellow and totally convinced that the world was a supremely beautiful place.

André made delightful company. He was easy to talk to, never allowed any pauses in the conversation, and their paths went back far enough to allow them to spend hours just chatting about people they knew in common.

'You're like a brother to me,' Alyssia said impulsively as they drove slowly back to the house around midnight.

'I've been told more flattering things before,' he responded, semi-serious.

'I'm not ready,' she said, 'for another relationship. You know that, don't you?' Actually, she thought, I'll never be ready for another relationship, but I'm not going to tell anyone that.

He nodded with a sigh. 'But we can still continue seeing each other while you're over here, can't we?'

'Sure,' Alyssia said. He reached out to hold her hand, and she let him. The physical contact between them did nothing for her at all, but it was nice all the same. Affectionate and comforting.

The car pulled up outside the house, and they walked to the door, still holding hands like a couple of children.

She was beginning to feel a little drowsy, a combination of the effect of the wine and the amount of food she had consumed.

Aggravating little thoughts were flitting somewhere in her head, but they weren't bothering her. They weren't connecting enough to be troublesome.

'Can I kiss you goodnight?' André asked. 'No strings attached.'

Why not? Alyssia thought happily. She lifted her face to his, and felt his lips on hers. They didn't fire a response in her, but it felt nice, like when they had been holding hands. Nice and unthreatening.

She leaned closer towards him, and half closed her eyes, and decided that really, if she tried hard enough, she might just be able to convince herself that Piers Morrison wasn't the only fish in the sea.

CHAPTER SEVEN

ANDRÉ, Alyssia discovered, proved to be alarmingly persistent in his promise to see her as much as possible while she remained in France.

And, of course, she acknowledged, who else could she blame but herself? She had made no effort to erect any 'keep off' signs, and their kiss the evening before had given him heaven only knew what sort of ideas.

She felt a bit like someone caught in quicksand, whose every turn only succeeded in further compounding the difficulties.

First Jonathan, which had been, in retrospect, a mere blemish on the horizon. Then Piers. She paused in applying her make-up and stared reflectively at the mirror. That was really where all the problems had begun. She had allowed her emotions to run wild over common sense and, now that she was well and truly embroiled in an impossible situation, found that her every reaction was triggered by her heart rather than her head.

Wasn't that partly the reason why she had agreed to see André in the first place? A misplaced need to prove to herself, and to Piers—even though he couldn't care less—that she could do as she liked? That he meant nothing to her?

When will I ever grow up? she frustratedly asked her reflection.

She wouldn't be here now, dressed to the nines for an evening that would be about as thrilling as an attack of flu, if she hadn't again responded in anger to her emotions.

She had almost successfully deterred André from his plans to paint the town red with her, had vaguely told him that she would see how she felt when he issued the invitation, only to pour all her good intentions down the drain when this morning Piers had received a call from Nicole, and informed Alyssia offhandedly that he would be out for the balance of the day.

He had barely glanced at her, and she had blurted out on the spur of the moment, 'Fine. Well, I probably won't see you till some time tomorrow. André and I are going to Monaco for the evening.'

She had planned on no such thing, but the mere thought of Piers with Nicole had made her see red, and her reaction had made her angrier still.

Every instinct in her told her not to care, but as she had looked at him she had been all too aware of his lean virility and of her responses to it.

So here I am now, she thought, shuddering. I hope André doesn't see this as a welcome mat for him to make any more advances. She had been stupid enough to have kissed him once, but tonight she would make sure that the mistake wasn't repeated.

Fiery Aries, she thought grimly. That had been the astrologer's description of her. Stupid Aries might have been more to the point, because the only person who seemed to have been burnt by her fire was herself.

She finished applying her make-up, the blusher making her cheekbones appear even higher than they were, her mouth full and tempting under the deep rose lip-gloss, her finely chiselled features lending her the appearance of an aristocrat.

Normally she would have derived great satisfaction from the image, and even greater satisfaction from the prospect of spending the night amid the pulsating excitement of Monaco at night, but right now she was finding it hard to work up even the tiniest bit of enthusiasm.

She slipped on a figure-hugging black dress and adorned the outfit with a bold selection of costume jewellery.

In those sort of casinos in the south of France, she thought, it would be in poor taste to adorn oneself with fake diamonds. Not when only the real thing was worn. But costume jewellery had the distinct advantage of not pretending to be anything other than what it was.

I'm going to have a good time, she told herself firmly when she heard André's knock on the door. And I won't spare a minute's thought for the fact that Piers hasn't been around for the entire day, and lord only knows what he's getting up to with Nicole. Somehow she doubted that preparing meals for the child and the husband featured very high on the agenda.

How she managed to get through the next few hours mystified her. All those things that had once appealed to every instinct inside her for excitement failed to arouse anything but a nagging desire to look at her watch and wonder what time she could reasonably convince André that it was time to leave.

They had dinner at a superb restaurant, bustling with the rich and famous, where everyone covertly glanced at everyone else, slyly assessing outfits and hairdos. She knew, with a feeling of detachment, that she attracted quite a few stares herself, primarily from men, and that if she had not had André at her side she would have been in very real danger of having to concoct a few efficient exit lines.

And André was in his element, enjoying the buzzing

atmosphere around him the way she had used to at one point in time.

She found herself half listening to his gossip, her mind drifting away to Piers and Nicole, wondering whether the day they were spending together had spilled over into night, and whether her husband suspected anything about what was between them.

She wondered what he was like. Old, perhaps? Too old to see that his wife was in love with someone else? Or perhaps one of these workaholics who only became aware of difficulties in their marriage when their wives had packed their bags and left their goodbye note on the mantelpiece?

'A spot of gambling before we leave?' André whispered in her ear, and Alyssia dragged herself away from her thoughts.

'Oh, André, must we?' She looked at her watch and realised with disappointment that it was much earlier than she had expected.

'I thought you enjoyed that sort of thing.'

'Not tonight.'

'It'll take your mind off things,' he said coaxingly.

'A good night's sleep would do that just as well,' she pointed out, and saw him pout disapprovingly.

'But sleeping's not nearly so much fun. Unless, of course——'

'Or,' she interrupted hastily, 'not nearly so expensive, for that matter.'

'What's money but pieces of paper?'

'I think there are quite a lot of people who wouldn't agree with you.' I sound like Piers, she thought suddenly, when a few months ago I would have giggled a bit at a remark like that. 'Oh, come on, then,' she said irritably, wanting to add, let's just get this fun evening over with.

He had already consumed more than one bottle of wine on his own, Alyssia managing to sip so slowly through her one glass that she was still stone-cold sober, and fully aware that at this rate her lift home would be out of the question and that she would more likely have to get a taxi.

André's delighted grin brought a resigned smile to her lips, and they caught a cab to one of the casinos, where the roulette tables were buzzing with that particular glittering breed of night-life whose adrenalin flowed in front of the gambling table.

Beautiful women, dressed in anything from the flamboyantly obvious to the understatedly elegant, weaved in and out of the crowds, some of them hanging on the arms of men old enough to be their grandfathers.

Everyone and everything breathed money. Alyssia wondered how she had ever managed to come to places such as this and accept it as part of everyday life.

No wonder Piers had been so contemptuous of her when they had first met. The trouble was that he couldn't begin to see how much she had changed.

Her head was beginning to throb from the smoky, claustrophobic atmosphere, and she wondered how she could tactfully drop a few hints about leaving without inviting a tirade of displeasure from André, which was the last thing she felt she could cope with.

He was having a wonderful time, and had at least, she noticed, retained enough good sense to make sure that his losses at the table were minimal.

At a little after one she informed him that she was ready to leave, her expression leaving him in no doubt that any objections on his part would be swiftly killed.

'But I can't drive you back,' he said apologetically.

Alyssia gave him a dry look. 'Tell me something I

hadn't already figured out for myself. I'll have to take a taxi.'

'What, at this hour?' He laughed outright. 'You'll be lucky. Let's just book into a hotel.'

'A hotel?'

'One of those things people stay in when they're not at home.'

'I know what a hotel is,' she snapped, pulling him outside into the fresh air, 'but——'

'But what?' He gave her a look that was penetratingly shrewd, considering the amount he had drunk. 'Don't tell me you're scared of offending the big bad wolf.'

'Of course not!'

'Or maybe he'll be jealous. Is that what you think?'

'Don't be ridiculous,' she protested, but his barb had struck home.

Why shouldn't she spend the night here and make her way back in the morning? She didn't have to account to Piers for her actions. He certainly didn't account to her for his!

So she found herself staying in a single room at one of the hotels in Monaco and the following morning making her way back to the cottage with a very much subdued André, whose head was feeling all the after-effects of too much wine.

She felt grubby, tired and, now that the car had pulled up outside the cottage, sickeningly tense. Which, she reminded herself, was ludicrous. The thought made her feel slightly better, but she still found herself tentatively letting herself in, relieved in a way that André was a bit under the weather.

It was all futile. Piers was in the living-room as they walked in, half naked, the top button of his faded jeans undone.

He looked up from the newspaper and looked coldly at them.

'I gather,' he drawled, 'you had a good time last night.'

Alyssia's eyes flashed. 'Great,' she muttered, her body stiffening as André slung his arm over her shoulders.

'Great,' he reiterated, 'sampled a bit of the local night-life, lost a few francs at the gambling tables, and then found that we couldn't drag ourselves away from each other, so we spent the night in a hotel.'

Alyssia gasped at his loose rendition of the truth, and then closed her mouth as she took in Piers's frozen expression.

She had almost been tempted to explain away André's remark, but her mind was working quickly. Just who did he think he was with that arrogant, contemptuous expression on his face? He didn't own her, did he? So she bit back her explanation, even though she could not bring herself to respond to André's embrace.

Piers carelessly tossed the newspaper on to the ground, then stretched out his long legs on the coffee-table, linking his fingers on his stomach.

'What a charitable gesture,' he said thoughtfully. 'Perhaps you could patent it. Sex as the cure-all for bouts of depression.'

'We——' Alyssia began.

'Certainly found it cured a few problems,' André finished for her. He knew that he was stirring things up; she could sense it in his voice.

'Or initiated a few,' Piers said smoothly, looking at André. 'You look as though you need a few days' sleep to recover from the night's activities.'

'Yes,' Alyssia jumped in, 'it's really time you left, André. Tell Simone I'll call her before I leave France.'

She shifted the weight of his arm from her shoulders and began urging him towards the front door before his fabrications began to get even more elaborate.

'I'll be in touch,' he said loudly before he left, and Alyssia shook her head in frustration, finding it difficult to be angry, even though he had blackened her yet more in Piers's eyes. She virtually shoved him towards his car.

She made her way back into the house, and was quite prepared to ignore Piers's presence on the sofa, when something made her stop.

She sat down awkwardly on one of the chairs, feeling highly incongruous in her black dress, which she had been obliged to put back on that morning, and looked down at her stiletto-clad feet.

'I'd like to explain a few things,' she began unsteadily, licking her lips.

'Would you? Why?'

He was making no effort to help her with this, but she was determined not to let that cold, impassive expression on his face browbeat her to the safety of her bedroom.

'It's not what it seems.'

'No?' He looked mildly interested. 'You mean, you didn't spend the night with him in a hotel?'

'No! I mean, yes!'

'You seem a little confused,' he said mildly. 'Perhaps your night of passion had addled you more than you think?'

'No, it hasn't!'

'Look, I have work to do, so. . .'

He stood up, but Alyssia hurriedly got to her feet,

walking across to him and urgently gripping his arm with her hand.

He was confusing her, sabotaging the lines of communication between them and making her sound even more guilty than she had to start with.

The warmth of his arm shot through her fingers.

'Please,' she said.

'OK.' He sat back down on the sofa with a bored expression on his face. 'So carry on. What exactly do you want to say?'

'André and I—you have the wrong impression of what happened between us last night.'

'Have I?' His grey eyes swept derisively over her and she flinched. 'How do you know what impression I have, and what makes you think that I give a damn what you and that boy get up to in your spare time?'

'We didn't get up to anything!' Alyssia shouted.

'Now, I wonder why I find that stretching the boundaries of my credibility.'

'You. . .!'

'Dammit, Alyssia,' he responded forcefully, 'you slept with me. Do you really expect me to believe that you wouldn't sleep with André as well? I don't flatter myself that I'm the only man on your horizon.'

'In that case, there's not much point to this conversation, is there?' she asked tautly. She could feel tears stinging the back of her eyes, but she would not let him see how vulnerable she was.

The astrologer had been right. She had been heading for trouble by ever imagining that this man could be touched like any normal human being.

Because he wasn't normal at all. There was a core of hardness to him that prevented him from ever responding to her.

'You want to believe the worst of me,' she accused

harshly, no longer caring what she said to him, or how much she was stoking his anger. 'You're rude, you're cynical, and I was a fool to ever make love to you.'

Her eyes glittered with unshed tears, but now they stemmed more from anger than misery.

His cold, controlled façade had slipped a little, and there was anger in his eyes now.

'Are you regretting making love to me,' he grated, 'or are you only regretting that you made love to me instead of saving yourself for André?'

'What do you think?'

'I'm asking you what you think!'

'I think,' she said, deliberately lowering the tone of her voice, which was bordering on the hysterical, 'that something happened to you in the past, you loved someone else, and it's turned you into a bitter man. At least I'm not bitter!'

What had she done now? She was horrified by her own admission, and even more horrified by the expression on his face and by the thick silence that greeted her statement.

Now, she thought, would be a highly opportune moment to make my departure.

She mustered up as much dignity as she possibly could and stood up, not chancing another look at Piers's face. She didn't need to catch his eyes now. Lord knew what that would have triggered off. No, a speedy and preferably silent retreat would give him time to calm down from her preposterous speculation on his private life.

At least she had not compounded her remark by backing it up with an astrologer's predictions. That, she thought, would definitely have been the match to ignite the dry wood.

She edged quietly towards the door, but didn't

manage to get further than the edge of the chair when she was pinned to the spot by fierce grey eyes.

'So that's how you spend your time, is it,' he grated, 'speculating with that fertile little imagination of yours on something that doesn't concern you whatsoever?'

Alyssia gasped at his denunciation of her. Every word was a calculated insult.

'If that's what you think then your ego is even bigger than I suspected!'

She turned around to race up to her bedroom, but anger and hurt forced her to spin back to face him.

'I wouldn't have done any speculating at all,' she informed him in a trembling voice, 'if you could bring yourself to be honest with me!'

'My past doesn't concern you. Because we made love, because I'm physically attracted to you, it doesn't mean that I owe you an involved explanation of my private life.'

His words were like a slap across her face. The blood rushed to her head, making her dizzy and totally incapable of finding anything snappy to retort.

Not that there was anything to retort. He was right. He didn't owe her a thing. The only reason it hurt so much was that she was so desperately in love with him.

Dignity right now seemed a bit optimistic, when she could feel her eyes blurring over with tears, but anything was better than standing here at the foot of the stairs, rooted to the spot and subjected mercilessly to his naked inspection of her.

She turned and bounded up the stairs, slamming the door behind her.

Then she threw herself on to the bed and stuck the pillow over her head, biting her teeth together, absolutely determined not to cry.

There was no way that she would give him the

satisfaction of seeing her emerge later in the evening with puffy red eyes.

As it was, she had made a big enough fool of herself already.

With her thoughts raging uncontrolled in her head, and the pillow muffling the noises outside, she was not aware of the door to her bedroom being opened at all.

The first she knew of Piers's presence in the room was his light touch on her shoulder, and it was so unexpected that she almost jumped a mile into the air.

'What do you want?' she asked mutinously, deliriously thankful that she had succeeded in not succumbing to the urge to blub her eyes out when she had dashed out of the living-room.

It would have done nothing for her already damaged ego if he had barged his way into her bedroom, only to find himself having to wade through a torrent of tears.

He stared down at her for a moment, then walked across to the window and began staring outside instead.

'Well?' she pressed him, sitting up and looking at the broad back facing her.

Still no response. Something in her flared.

'Look,' she bit out, 'if you. . .you took it upon yourself to waltz into my bedroom, *uninvited*, merely to admire the scenery then I'd appreciate it if you'd kindly waltz back out. You can appreciate the scenery from another window in another room.' Or preferably she thought, from another house altogether.

For the first time she had met him a flush darkened the back of his neck.

'I shouldn't have said some of the things that I did,' he muttered.

It was, she realised with astonishment, his version of an apology, and she had a feeling that it had taken a lot out of him to say it.

She knew that she should extend some kind of apology herself, but she knew equally well that she had no intention of doing any such thing. Se had blurted out one or two things which, admittedly, were none of her business, but she certainly wasn't sorry about that. She was only sorry that she had demonstrated exactly how vulnerable she was to him.

'Fine,' she conceded tersely, 'now that you've got that off your chest, you're free to leave.'

He turned around to face her and approached the bed.

'You bring out the worst in me, woman,' he said, leaning over her and supporting himself on his hands, one on either side of her head, trapping her.

Panic gripped her. From this close, he could turn her blood to water, her brain to cotton wool, and he was, even though she was trying hard to fight it.

'Not much I can say to that, is there?' she managed bravely, wishing desperately that he would straighten up and go his merry way.

She didn't need this continual somersaulting of her emotions. No sooner had she begun manufacturing a few defences than he demolished them with a flick of his finger. She knew how Sisyphus must have felt, rolling that stone wearily up the hill, only to see it slide back down again as he made it to the top.

'I like it when you're not talking,' he agreed, and gave her a look of scorching intimacy.

This time the panic was replaced by a sensation of falling through air. She half closed her eyes, but she knew that the picture she presented was anything but detached. Her face was flushed, her hair a tumbled mass on the pillow, her breathing quick and uneven, drawing attention to the rise and fall of her breasts.

When he brushed some hair away from her face he

might just as well have placed his hand on her most intimate spot. She moaned weakly, inviting him unknowingly to kiss her pouting lips.

When he did, his mouth ravaging hers a peculiarly sweet fierceness, pressing her head back against the pillow, she shuddered uncontrollably and, after a moment's hesitation, twined her hands behind his head, pulling him down until he was lying on top of her.

She felt as though she couldn't get enough of him, and in that split instant she made her decision.

She couldn't fight this any longer. If he wanted her, even if it was only to satiate a temporary need, even if she was only a substitute for the woman he really wanted, then she would oblige, because he had reduced her will-power to nothing.

'God,' he muttered against her neck, 'you can be the most impossible woman I've ever met, but I want you so badly that it hurts.'

'Yes,' she murmured in a quick, husky voice. 'I want you, too.'

She arched back, and his mouth travelled along her neck, his teeth nipping her skin.

Their clothes were an abrasive barrier between them, and her hands were as urgent as his as she peeled off the same black dress she seemed to have been wearing for the past century.

Then he divested her of her stockings, tossing them into a shimmering heap on the floor.

She watched, mesmerised, as he undressed himself, drinking in the strong lines of his body, aware that her absorption was delighting him.

'I want to spend the rest of the day making love to you,' he murmured, biting her ear, 'I want to touch every part of your body.'

He was teasing her with this leisurely foreplay, stoking the fires inside her until they reached the point where they could no longer be contained.

She stroked his body, feeling a sense of power at his groan of appreciation.

When he touched her, her flesh burnt. He trailed his fingers along her breasts, feeling the nipples harden in expectation, and she lay back, breathing quickly, her body turning to liquid under his hands.

With a deep moan of pleasure she guided his head to her breasts, arching back as she felt his mouth wetly caressing them.

She knew that he was as fiercely aroused as she was, but he was taking his time, enjoying her.

He sucked at her breasts, tasting them, then her stomach, and with every feel of his mouth she thought that she would explode.

'Please,' she murmured shakily.

Their bodies joined in rhythmic unison, and she thought with a swift, delirious stab of pleasure, How can any man ever compare with you?

He was transporting her to another world, and she responded to him with uninhibited abandon. Her hands grasped his back, and she could feel it wet with a thin film of perspiration.

They were moving in a timeless hemisphere, and it was with a deep feeling of contentment that she descended back into reality.

When he lay down beside her she impulsively turned to him.

'I don't want commitment, Piers,' she lied, 'any more than you do. But I want you. I want you every minute of every day that I'm here with you.' The words were out. She was offering herself to him on a silver platter, no strings attached, and she would simply cope with the agony of their parting when the time came.

He stroked her face, and then ran his fingers through her hair, looking at it as if it were made of some delicate, finely spun silk.

She could feel his heart beating steadily under the palm of her hand, and looked into his eyes, gazing down at her.

'That's enough for you?' he asked softly.

'It's enough,' she whispered, looking away from his intense stare in case he read the truth in her eyes and recoiled from it.

He had warned her that desire was all he had to offer her, and he had probably assumed that his warning had hit home. It would hardly cross his mind that she had gone past the point of that to something altogether more serious and far less retrievable.

She tried to stifle the insidious army of questions tentatively beginning to attack her.

What was going to happen when her little jaunt in France was over, for instance? She only had two days left, and the thought of nothing after that made her shiver with dread. She never thought that she would look at emptiness and not immediately be able to think of a hundred ways of filling it.

This time the chasm yawned in front of her, and she knew that she might close her eyes for the moment, but she was already taking little steps towards the edge.

He rolled her on to her back and kissed her, his hand massaging her breast, teasing the nipple into arousal.

Alyssia's roundabout attempts to find answers to some of her questions died on her lips.

She closed her eyes, enjoying the sensations flooding her as his hands parted her legs, and his breathing became as erratic as hers.

'When I first saw you,' he murmured into her ear, 'I made the mistake of thinking that you were the eternal butterfly. Flitting from one flower to the next, whichever looked the most tempting, but totally incapable of feeling any real passion. God, I couldn't have been more wrong.'

This time there was no prolonged foreplay. They made love as though tomorrow was fast approaching, and with it imminent departure. It matched her mood, and her movements against him were desperate with hunger.

No one could have warned her about him, she thought. He had sprung out at her from nowhere, not even giving her the time to brace herself against him.

Men, she thought; who needs them?

They had always been such an uncomplicated species before she had met Piers. They smiled, flattered, charmed, and she smiled back willingly, but remained unmoved.

It had all been an enjoyable game, and she had always imagined that love would be an enjoyable game as well, except that there was nothing enjoyable about the pain eating away at her. Worse, she preferred the pain of being with him and knowing that he didn't return her feelings to the pain of not being with him at all.

This was, she knew, thinking back to what the astrologer had said all that time ago in London, the blaze that had been ignited and over which she had no control.

There was just one thing now that she had to find out.

'Piers,' she whispered hesitantly, 'what's your star sign?'

He raised his eyebrows in surprise. 'If you must know,' he said lazily, 'it's Virgo.'

Beware, she thought with a stab of coldness, the Virgo threat.

Wasn't it too late now?

CHAPTER EIGHT

NORMALLY the trip to St Tropez would have been
Alyssia's idea, but when, the following morning, Piers
suggested it her only reaction was to wince with
distaste.

'Must we?' she asked. 'I can think of a thousand
better things to do.' She threw her arms around Piers
where he was sitting at the breakfast table, and nipped
his neck with her teeth.

'I can guess what you have in mind,' he said drily.

'Would you prefer more subtlety?' she asked. 'A few
coy looks, fluttering eyelashes, all that sort of thing?'

'I don't know,' he drawled, 'I'd probably be too
surprised by coy looks from you to have any idea what
they were leading up to.'

'Meaning?'

'Meaning that directness is more often your
approach.'

He stood up and stretched, and Alyssia's eyes followed the contours of his lean body, with the faded
denims and short-sleeved T-shirt.

Ever since they had made love the night before she
had wanted nothing more than to continue touching
him. In fact, she would have ideally wanted them to
spend the next day and a half in bed together, and
hang the consequences. After all, what was going to
happen after that? He had not mentioned any future to
their relationship, not even a future of a temporary
nature, and she was reluctant to broach the subject.

Alyssia wrinkled her nose in mock hurt.

'I don't know whether to take that remark as a compliment or not,' she said dubiously.

Piers grinned down at her, his eyebrows raised.

'Stick on a swimsuit, and we'll take our chances on the car making it there in one piece.'

'I never wear a swimsuit when I go to St Tropez,' she said a little petulantly.

'Make this the exception.'

She went upstairs and slung her bikini bottoms in a bag, along with her suntan oil and a towel, and ran downstairs, to find him waiting for her by the front door.

So what if he didn't want to spend the day cooped up with her in the bedroom, only emerging when hunger demanded that their stomachs be fed? It was enough just to be with him.

She felt as though she was on a high. She didn't want to have to think of the consequences of it. She wanted to postpone any thoughts of coming back down to reality for as long as possible.

She remembered St Tropez as being vibrant. Now, with her bag slung over her shoulder and her sunglasses propped firmly on her nose, it struck her as simply crowded.

'I can't imagine why you wanted to come here,' she said, staring at the milling crowds of people with distaste.

Piers shrugged and looked at her. 'This is the sort of life you've been brought up to enjoy. Glamour, chic cafés and discothèques. You should be in your element.'

He had a point. She used to enjoy it, but couldn't he tell that she had changed?

Obviously not. Maybe this was his little way of reminding her that she was not really his type of woman. That Nicole was his type of woman and always would be. Maybe, she thought with an acrobatic leap of logic, this was by way of telling her that she should start acclimatising herself to her old way of life, because that was where she would be in less than two days' time.

'I suppose I should,' she said non-committally.

They browsed for a while through the streets.

Alyssia didn't care how she looked. She was wearing a pair of off-white trousers, which she had cuffed as much as she could at the ankles because of the heat, and a plain navy-coloured T-shirt, neither of which sported designer labels.

She felt gloriously immune to the unspoken pull here to wear the right clothes, to be seen with the right people, in the right places, at the right time.

I've really changed, she thought ironically. Two weeks in a semi-finished house, with a man who doesn't give a damn about appearances have worked their magic, and I don't know if I'm Cinderella now or the pumpkin, but I'm certainly not the obnoxious girl who arrived here a fortnight ago.

She turned to find Piers staring at her, and she suddenly said, 'Penny for them.'

'My thoughts?'

She nodded, linking her fingers through his, loving the warmth of his strong, capable hand.

'If you really want to know, I was thinking how much I hate crowds, despite the fact that my job involves a lot of travelling.'

She frowned, thinking that he was trying to tell her something, but what? And the moment was lost as a couple of motorcyclists roared by.

'I was also thinking,' he whispered softly into her ear, 'that I could find a secluded spot and make love with you right now, if such a thing as a secluded spot existed in this place.'

Alyssia's pulses raced in response to his words and their seductive intimacy.

What on earth had Nicole been thinking to have married someone else?

'Don't.' She blushed, smiling.

'Failing that,' he said pragmatically, 'shall we meander into a café for something to drink?'

'Why not?' The thought of a long, cold drink and a brief respite from the crowded streets was tempting.

They found a café down a side-street, and were about to find somewhere to sit when she heard a voice call out to Piers. A very familiar voice. She looked around and saw Nicole behind her, smiling and on the arm of a very distinguished silver-haired man, presumably her husband. Although, she thought with uncharitable spitefulness, he was old enough to be her father.

It dawned on her for the first time that perhaps the other woman had married for money. Perhaps Piers had been no more than a struggling architect when they had first met, and she had not been content to lead a life of poverty.

Now that he was rich, she was tied.

The scenario had such an element of truth about it that she found herself embroidering details. He had been bitter to start with, but love was blind. He still couldn't resist her, even if he might be too honourable to sleep with her.

'Join us,' Nicole said, and Alyssia thought, Of all the people in the world to meet, why her? Why did she have to appear on the scene and spoil everything?

She was impeccably dressed, and on a stiflingly hot day still managed to look coolly coiffured, every hair in place, her make-up none the worse for the heat. She might not be beautiful, but she wore her clothes with typical French panache.

Alyssia blew some of the flyaway blonde strands away from her face and followed them to a small table at the back of the café, hoping that she would not have to endure half an hour of French conversation while she sat on the sidelines, wondering whether what they were discussing was really as animated and interesting as it appeared.

Fortunately she didn't. The silver-haired gentleman, who turned out to be fluent in English and very charming in a gracious sort of way, chatted to her amiably about the south of France, though Alyssia didn't miss the way his eyes wandered unconsciously across to his wife every so often.

Obviously, she thought sourly, checking to make sure that no hanky-panky was going on under the table between Piers and her, or else he was still so infatuated that he couldn't bear not to look at her for too long.

Her opinion of Nicole dropped a further few notches.

Alyssia refused to give in to any urge to stare at Piers, though she was sorely tempted. After all, she didn't own Piers Morrison, he could talk to just whom-ever he pleased, and she was in no mood to hear any amused remarks from him afterwards about jealousy.

'And how is your child?' she asked when there was a break in the conversation, wondering whether that friendly mask would slip and a bit of guilt might seep through.

But it didn't. Nicole looked quite thrilled to have been asked the question, and she haltingly explained that her son was at a party and that they would be collecting him later that morning.

'The proud mother,' her husband said indulgently.

'So I see,' Alyssia replied in a stiff voice, wondering what was going on in Piers's head at this masquerade.

All the feelings that had taken a back seat since they had slept together resurfaced, and she suddenly felt lost and confused.

'And you want the children some day?' Nicole asked interestedly.

Alyssia gave her a coldly polite stare. 'Some day, perhaps,' she said, 'but at the moment I'm far too busy enjoying my single life.' There seemed little point in launching into the saga of her engagement, and it also seemed like an ideal opportunity to tell Piers obliquely that she wasn't emotionally involved with him.

More coffee was ordered, and general conversation resumed.

Who would have imagined that everyday life was so strewn with consummate actors? she thought bitterly. No one would have guessed that Piers and Nicole were involved, least of all her husband.

She was relieved when Nicole stood up.

Her hand was reaching for her bag when the other woman asked her, in her delightfully broken English, to accompany her to a boutique across the road and give her an opinion on a dress she wanted to buy.

'We leave the boys for a while, *non*?'

Oh, God, Alyssia thought, help.

She didn't want to accompany Nicole anywhere, and she doubted whether the other woman really needed any advice from her on clothes anyway.

But what could she do? Piers was grinning, and, short of making a fool of herself, she had no option but to smile weakly at them and concur.

She reluctantly followed Nicole outside, certain that she was verging on dragging her steps and generally acting like a twelve-year-old delinquent on the way to the principal's office.

They went into the boutique, Alyssia barely glancing at the racks of exquisitely made clothes, nodding distractedly in agreement when Nicole picked out an exotic pink strapless dress and asked whether she thought it would suit her.

Her stomach was doing weird things, and she was about to launch into some inane chit-chat to take her mind off the sensation when Nicole, while paying for the dress, said to her, 'Actually, I want to speak with you.'

'Did you?' Alyssia said, alarmed. 'I mean, do you?'

'You do not mind, do you?'

'Mind?' Alyssia forced a don't-be-silly expression on to her face. 'Why should I mind?' Then she added for good measure, 'I don't know what you want to talk to me about, do I?'

'About Piers.'

'Oh.' Who else? She would hardly have dragged her into this boutique if she had wanted a simple discussion on the weather or the price of vegetables.

'I gather you two are—what is the word?— involved?'

'In a manner of speaking,' Alyssia said reluctantly. She didn't know where this conversation was leading, but gut feeling told her that she could bank on the destination's being rather unpleasant.

Nicole smiled.

Friendly enough, but then crocodiles seemed to smile. And they were hardly the friendliest creatures on the face of the earth.

Alyssia bared her teeth in a semblance of a smile and then abandoned the effort. It made her feel as if she should be sharpening her sword in preparation.

'Ah. I was right. It is easy for a woman to spot these things, you agree?'

'Is it?'

'I think so, but maybe that's being French, *non*? Maybe the English sometimes miss what is in front of the nose.'

'You make us sound like a nation of cabbages.'

'Cabbages?'

'Stupid.'

'Ah.' Nicole smiled. 'But I do not mean to!'

'Anyway. . .you were saying?'

There was a pause while Nicole paid the bill, putting it on her husband's gold credit card, then she straightened up and picked up the bag.

'We go for a short walk, *non*?'

Must we? Alyssia wanted to ask, but she didn't. She fell in with Nicole's steps, watching as she gesticulated to the men, letting them know that they wouldn't be long.

'Yes, I want to speak with you about Piers. He is different now, you know? Perhaps you do not see it, but he and I. . .'

'I know. The two of you go back a long way.' If this were a musical, she thought irrelevantly, there'd be a song about now.

'He told you?' Nicole stared at her interestedly, and for a minute Alyssia was disconcerted. Shouldn't the reaction at this point be freezing anger?

She knew that that would be what she would feel if the roles were reversed.

'He told me.'

'And what else did he tell you?'

She shrugged casually, hating to spoil the impression of intimacy between herself and Piers by confessing that he had told her nothing.

'Nothing' she was constrained to admit, rather than tell an out and out lie, however tempting the lie was.

Nicole looked disappointed.

'So he does not speak of us, then? Our relationship to one another?'

'You're related?' Alyssia asked hopefully.

Nicole burst out laughing. '*Mais non! Au contraire.* I mean, we have a special relationship, and I was hoping that he would have talked with you about that. It's been such a long time, too long. . .' She stopped talking, as though she had already said too much and was regretting it.

'You were saying?' Alyssia ventured. 'Why don't you tell me about it?' She stopped walking and stood still, folding her arms resolutely across her chest. 'I hate all these riddles. They're beginning to give me a headache.'

'You have a headache? I have some tablets.'

Alyssia narrowed her eyes, wondering whether this was an unexpected wisecrack from the other woman, but she realised that Nicole had merely taken her literally and was now rummaging in her bag for the tablets.

'No,' Alyssia said, grinning despite herself, 'I was speaking figuratively. What I mean is my headache's gone.'

Nicole's face cleared. 'So we return to the men, *non*?'

'Tell me what's going on between you and Piers,' she heard herself pleading as she walked beside her.

'What is going on? It's a strange expression, but *non*, I cannot tell you that. It must come from Piers.'

So that, Alyssia thought wearily, is that. The only positive thing that had come out of the conversation had been Nicole's offer of some aspirin.

That and the fact that she had managed to stir all those self-doubts that had been hovering at the back of her mind.

Look, a little voice told her, he hasn't mentioned commitment, true enough. In fact, it continued, he hasn't even mentioned what will happen after you catch the next plane back to Heathrow.

She was quiet as they made their way to the beach, which was every bit as packed as she had known it would be.

St Tropez was known for its beaches, and normally she could spend hours just soaking up the sun and watching the other people parading, but she felt too unsettled to do much more than lie on her towel, playing aimlessly with the sand and trying to convince herself that she did not want anything more out of Piers than he was prepared to give her.

She watched as he stretched out his towel alongside her, and it didn't escape her that she wasn't the only female on the beach who found him attractive.

His lean brand of nonchalant sexuality was attracting quite a few appreciative glances.

'Is this a regular haunt of yours?' she asked him a little waspishly.

'Well, no. Why?' He peered at her from under the cloth cap which he was using to shade his face, and she lay on her side to face him.

'Because the place is littered with women who all look as though they might know you, or else, if they don't, would like to.'

He grinned at her.

'Are you trying to tell me something about my sex appeal?'

'I'm not. But I think they might be,' she said disgruntledly. So what if he hasn't mentioned commit-

ment, she thought. I accepted this on his terms, didn't
I?

He reached behind her head and pulled her towards
him, kissing her lingeringly on her lips.

'I don't normally go in for public displays of affection,' he murmured, 'but you're irresistible. Not,' he
added wryly, 'that I should tell you that. Your head
will get even bigger than it already is.'

Are you seeing me or are you seeing her? She shoved
the thought to the very back of her mind.

'You make me sound like someone who spends their
entire day in front of the nearest mirror and never
travels without a cosmetic tray in their handbag.'

'Funny you should mention it.'

She relaxed slightly and jabbed him in his ribs.

'I'm not like that,' she said huffily, 'and you're very
rude to even hint that I might be. I admit that I once
cared a hell of a lot about my appearance, but I've
changed.'

She was toying with the sand, scooping it up and
letting it trail through her fingers, and she didn't see
the expression in his eyes when he next spoke.

'People don't change overnight, Alyssia,' he said,
half joking but mostly serious. 'You can't erase a
lifetime of habit by spending two weeks in the
sunshine.'

'You don't know that,' she replied evenly. 'You can't
say that as though it's a fact.'

'I know I can't, but I can make inspired guesses.'

'In other words, you don't think I've changed one
bit.' The thought hurt.

'Maybe you have,' he said, his tone lightening.

'What a generous admission. It's nice to know that
you're giving me the benefit of the doubt.'

He grinned, giving her a full dose of his masculine

charm, and she kissed him, lingeringly, just as he had kissed her.

'I don't normally go in for public displays of affection either,' she murmured impulsively, forgetting her uneasiness, 'but even with sand on your face you're. . .'

'Irresistible?'

'Something like that.' Something very much like that, she thought with sudden sadness. He would not begin to guess just how much she loved and wanted him, because he felt nothing of the sort for her. To him, she was still the same Alyssia, and heaven only knew why he had slept with her.

No, she knew the reason. He was a man and she had hardly fought him off. Just the opposite. She might just as well have stuck a neon sign on her head, inviting him to make love to her.

What was it he had said? That she favoured the direct approach? Her attraction to him had hardly been swathed in subtlety.

And, in the absence of the woman he really wanted, why should he fight her off?

They swam and lazed on the beach, having a light lunch from one of the huts along the beach that served food, and drove back to the house towards the end of the evening in silence, Alyssia preoccupied with her thoughts.

'Do you travel much?' she asked suddenly.

'What an odd question.' Piers shot her a puzzled look. 'Yes, I do. Why?'

'Where to? Here?'

'A fair amount, I suppose. Where are these questions leading?'

'Nowhere.' She looked out of the window at the fast-approaching twilight. A magical hour, especially here,

with the trees swaying at the side of the road, and
everything looking vaguely blurred and drowsy.

'Really?' he said. 'They seemed rather laden to me,
but I'll take your word for it if you tell me that it's all
general interest in my private life.'

'Private life?' A note of bitterness crept into her
voice. 'I thought that that was barred off to the likes of
me.' I'm spoiling everything, she thought, but she
couldn't help herself. Every time she thought about
how much he kept hidden behind that sexy face of his
her blood went cold.

'The likes of you?' His voice had hardened
imperceptibly.

'A bed companion.'

'I thought that we had sorted all that out.'

'We have,' she agreed numbly, fishing around for
something amazingly trivial to say that would lighten
the atmosphere.

'Then why do I get the distinct impression that we're
going round and round in the same circles?'

She shrugged. 'Beats me.'

They had reached the house, but when she made a
move to open her door he leant across and slammed it
shut.

'What the hell has got into you?'

'Nothing.' She licked her lips nervously and tried to
simulate deep interest in the scenery outside, which
was difficult, since there was very little to see in the
rapidly failing light.

'I'm beginning to read a wealth of meaning into that
monosyllable. Every time you say that, what you really
seem to mean is that there's a hell of a lot wrong but
you're not prepared to discuss it.'

'In which case, why are you trying to discuss it?'

Don't tell me that you care what the hell is on my mind, she thought to herself.

Things had been ticking along nicely between them, just as long as she'd been prepared to forget that she wanted more out of the relationship than a roll in the hay and a bright 'cheerio' at the airport.

With agonising clarity she realised that she couldn't fool herself that she would be content with that and, however tempting it was to take what he had to offer, no questions asked, it wasn't good enough for her. It left too many spaces saturated with hurt. And seeing Nicole had only reminded her of that fact.

From an easygoing girl she had metamorphosised into someone who wanted the proverbial all-or-nothing relationship. It would be laughable if it weren't so desperately painful.

How could this have happened to her? She, who had always pulled the strings, to have found herself in this position. Just when you least expect it, she thought, poetic justice is waiting right around the corner. Holding a rolling pin and determined to have the last laugh.

Piers was staring at her, and he finally caught her chin in his hand and turned her to face him.

'Are you going to stop sitting there like some god-dammed statue and fill me in on what's going on in your head?'

'Why?' she asked rashly. 'Do you care?'

'Ah, so that's it, is it?' He released her and sat back, flexing his legs in the confines of the car.

'Ah, so what's it?'

'You claim to be perfectly satisfied to enjoy what we have, when in fact you're looking for commitment.'

'I am not looking for commitment!'

'No? Don't tell me that you're bored already, then.'

'Bored?' He had unwittingly thrown her a life-jacket

and she grabbed it gratefully. 'Yes, I'm bored. Going to Nice and St Tropez showed me that it's time to leave all this rustic charm and get back to what I know.'

'I see.'

'I guess I threw myself at you because of everything that had happened between Jonathan and myself; I guess I was just looking for a diversion and you happened to be in the right place at the right time.'

'What a lucky fellow I am.'

Alyssia bit her lip until she felt a trickle of blood on her mouth. 'Face it, we used each other and——'

'And, now that you've got what you wanted, you might as well pack your bags and leave.'

'Something like that.'

'Well,' and she flinched at the cutting acidity in his voice, 'I never thought I'd see the day when a woman could fool me, but you managed pretty well. Now I know what you should do with all that free time you have: acting. Because you can damn well act the pants off anyone I've ever met in my life before.'

This is awful, Alyssia thought. Like slowly rubbing salt into an open wound.

'Don't tell me that you give a damn,' she said, 'don't tell me that I've been anything to you but a brief interlude.'

'If you say so.' His voice was no longer hard or angry. It was indifferent, and that was even worse.

'Now I think I'd better go and pack my things,' she mumbled.

She swung open her door, half hoping that something would happen, that fortune would toss some unforeseen card at her that would alter everything between them, but nothing happened.

'Aren't you coming in?' she asked timidly. She looked through the window at his profile.

He didn't turn to face her when he spoke. 'I can think of better things to do than share a house with a bitch like you. Even if it is for only one night more. So, if you wouldn't mind stepping back, I'll bid you goodbye. It's been an enlightening experience.'

He gave her a mocking salute, started the engine and, before she could find anything to say, was driving away from her.

Away from her and out of her life, for good. She waited until the car vanished round the bend then waited some more until the whine of the engine was at last lost in the distance, then she slowly made her way into the house.

It might feel it, she said to herself, but it wasn't the end of the world. The sun would still rise and still set regardless of the fact that she would never see him again. And she'd survive. No one ever died of a broken heart.

CHAPTER NINE

THE sunshine when she landed at Heathrow was a cruel reminder to Alyssia of the lazy days in France she had thought would never end.

She had left the house earlier that morning with the miserable feeling that things could never be right for her again.

She told herself that things could have been worse. At least Piers had not been around when she had left. He had spent the night away. Where, she didn't care to speculate on.

His absence had, at any rate, spared her the agony of facing the tight-lipped cynicism of his stares and that irreparable barrier that had sprung up between them in what had seemed like a matter of minutes.

She had awakened early, busied herself with her bags and, while she had waited for the taxi repeatedly told herself that men were a species that she would avoid at all costs from here on in.

It would have been just her luck if the damned thing had broken down *en route*, leaving her at the mercy of his unexpected return.

But the taxi had showed up on the dot, and she had stepped in, resolutely refusing to look back for one last glance at the house.

As soon as she got back to London she phoned Simone in a bout of maudlin self-pity and told her everything that had happened between them and her decision to end the relationship. Misery was always so much more manageable if it was poured into a friend's sympathetic ear.

'I came to my senses,' she said, economising with the truth until she felt more capable of handling it with any degree of calm.

'Really?' Simone said in a disbelieving tone of voice. 'That was remarkably quick. At the risk of having you bellow down the phone to me that it's none of my business, I think you made a big mistake. You two definitely had something going. I could sense it. I must be psychic.'

'Well, it went,' Alyssia said abruptly, and brought the subject to a speedy conclusion, realising that unburdening herself was doing nothing to ease her misery after all.

And, she realised, the very last thing she needed was a post-mortem on a failed relationship, especially when the relationship had been so horribly one-sided.

She spent the remainder of the week drifting aimlessly from room to room in the house, until her father irritably asked her one evening whether she had nothing better to do.

'Nothing springs to mind,' Alyssia said with an attempt at light-heartedness.

If this was any indication as to how she would be spending her time in London then she would have to find something to do, and quick. It had been bad enough lying to Piers, leaving him because she knew that she had to, however much she disliked it, but to while away her time here, doing nothing but mulling over past events, was a recipe for misery.

Of course, she argued with herself, she would feel miserable. She had been deeply in love with Piers, and still was. She could not clear her head of him, however much she told herself that he was a bastard. But wasn't that to be expected?

Time would solve everything, or at least it was supposed to. The books all said so.

Nevertheless, from where she was standing, all she could see was the endless succession of days, stretching into infinity, all of them empty and without meaning.

She had not realised before exactly how dependent she had become on Piers. Now she knew.

Without him around the energy to do even the simplest of chores had been taken away from her.

Telephoning Jonathan to break off the engagement had almost been a high point of comic relief. And cowardly. But she had not felt able to face anyone, least of all him.

And thankfully, after the initial shock, he had handled the situation better than she had expected. Although, she reasoned realistically, if he had been fooling around behind her back it indicated that what he felt for her fell very far short of love, in which case he would probably have cancelled the wedding if she hadn't.

In due course, she knew that she would have to pull herself together. She could hardly hide behind the four walls of her father's house for the rest of her life, but the mere thought of re-entering any sort of social scene was enough to make her feel ill.

You've ruined me, Piers Morrison, she thought angrily, staring at her reflection in the mirror as the prospect of a dreary Saturday evening faced her; I might not have been terribly nice before I met you, but at least I wasn't filled with this pain and dissatisfaction.

On a sudden impulse she declared to her father that she was going out.

'Good idea,' he said immediately from where he was

enjoying a leisurely read of the newspaper. 'I can't bear to see you moping around here any longer. Why the long face, anyway?'

'I'm not moping. Just bored,' she lied.

'I can think of a cure for that.'

'What?'

'Find yourself a job, or at least a hobby that you enjoy doing. It would be infinitely superior to those friends of yours.'

'Daddy, darling,' Alyssia said, smiling genuinely for the first time since she had stepped foot back on to English soil and kissing him on the tip of his nose, 'in your own cantankerous way, you've put your finger right on the button.'

Her father grinned at her from over the rim of his spectacles. 'Fathers are always right.'

'I thought it was mothers.'

'In the absence of mothers.'

She knew where she was going, and she wasted no time in getting there. The art shop in Covent Garden was the largest she could think of offhand, and the minute she walked in she knew that she had done the right thing.

She would paint Piers Morrison out of her system.

She took her time choosing the paints, the pad, the brushes, and then returned to the house in a fever of excitement.

She could hardly wait to start. She could recall his hard masculine looks with such clarity of detail that she didn't think that she would have any problem in recreating the image on paper.

And painting him would help to exorcise him. She hoped. Because the memories plaguing her were sending her quietly crazy, and it had only been a week since she had been out of his company.

She set to work with a vengeance, losing herself in the difficult task of making all those fiercely vivid images of him that were swirling around in her head tangible.

As the days meandered into each other she found herself spending all her free time painting, even though she had known almost from the start that painting him was not going to exorcise him.

If anything, it made his absence more startlingly real for her.

She did a series of sketches, trying to capture all his moods, thinking that, though they weren't very professional, they were to her, because she could see in every one of them all those complicated, aggravating, irresistible facets that made up his personality.

He had infuriated her, puzzled her, and finally won her over, and every time she looked over what she had painted her stomach lurched, and she knew without doubt that she would never forget him.

She was absorbed in her painting when her father interrupted her to tell her that there was a phone call for her.

'Who is it?' she asked warily, her brain trying to work out some excuse if it was one of her friends.

'Not a clue,' he said unhelpfully.

'Male or female?'

'Honestly, darling. Anyone would think that you were practising to become a hermit!' He walked back downstairs with Alyssia dragging her feet in his wake.

'Hello,' she said cautiously into the mouthpiece.

The voice down the line was instantly recognisable, and instantly unwelcome.

Alyssia felt her hairs stand on end as she heard that broken French accent.

'It is me—Nicole. You remember me?'

Remember you? Alyssia thought. Severe amnesia couldn't make me forget you. 'Yes,' she said tightly. 'What do you want?'

'I hope I do not disturb you by telephoning you; I find out you live in London from Piers, and so I think to myself that I will phone.'

Alyssia took a sharp intake of breath. Nearly two weeks without his name crossing her lips, and her emotions were still frighteningly close to the surface.

'You still haven't told me the purpose of this call,' Alyssia pointed out, deciding to put an end to this surface veneer of politeness.

'I am here, in London, and I think we can meet up, perhaps?'

'What for?'

'To talk.'

'We already have.' Or rather, she wanted to say, you talked and ruined my life, I listened and wished that I hadn't.

'We really need to discuss things.' There was a marked pause down the line. 'Please. Is important. Very important.'

'All right,' Alyssia conceded wearily, curious to hear what the other woman had to say, in spite of herself, 'where do you want to meet?'

She expected Nicole to name a restaurant, but instead she named the hotel where she was staying, one of the more expensive hotels in London, and they arranged to meet up that afternoon, in her room.

'Wouldn't you rather meet in the lobby?' Alyssia asked, puzzled, although she could not put her finger on why. 'We could go to a café or something. I have endless appointments, so I really can't stay long.'

'No,' Nicole said quickly, 'I mean, is more convenient if you come to the hotel. Say, around five? You won't be long if you do not wish.'

She only realised how tense she had been when she replaced the receiver and found the palm of her hands covered in a fine film of perspiration.

She still had a few hours of useful painting time left, but now she could not concentrate.

There were too many questions reverberating in her head.

By four o'clock she was ready, dressed in a light rose-pink skirt and slim-fitting top, and staring at her watch, anxiously counting the minutes to when she could reasonably leave and arrive on time.

It frustrated her that, after all her careful reasoning, the memory of him, lazy and powerful and sensuous, still had the power to make her tremble.

Wasn't that why, she told herself, she had agreed to see Nicole? Because she was a link to him, however hurtful that link was?

As she hurried to grab a taxi to the hotel she could feel her stomach coiling into knots of dread.

At rush-hour, the traffic was at a slow crawl, to the point where she was convinced that it would have been quicker simply to walk. The uncustomary heat didn't help matters either, nor did the taxi driver's attempt at jovial small talk, most of which Alyssia either ignored or answered in monosyllables.

She made her way up to the hotel bedroom and was let in by one of the porters.

'Mrs Giraud has asked us to tell you that she had to step out for a short while, but to make yourself at home,' the receptionist had informed her.

'Stepped out?' Alyssia had looked at the girl in amazement, beginning to feel disproportionately angry at this unexpected anticlimax.

She walked into the room feeling thoroughly deflated.

There was an ice bucket in the middle and a bottle of chilled champagne.

A drink? At this early hour of the evening? Either some folly on the part of the hotel, or else Nicole had a streak of insanity running through her. It was hardly as though they were friends, for heaven's sake.

She refused the porter's offer to crack open the bottle, and settled herself for a long wait.

I could be here indefinitely, she thought dismally.

She studied the room, taking in the luxurious décor, the tasteful old furniture, no doubt the same in every single room and almost certainly not genuine, but impressive nevertheless.

There was a compact flowered sofa in one corner, and she sat on it, trying to find something absorbing to do in a hotel room that was deprived of any literature apart from the hotel menu and some self-congratulatory stuff about the hotel itself.

Apart from that, it looked totally unlived-in.

She got up and checked the wardrobes, and her bemusement became sheer bewilderment.

There were no clothes, nothing.

In fact, no indication that anyone was staying there at all.

For a moment she felt a surge of panic. What if it had not been Nicole on the phone at all? What if it had been some lunatic who sounded like her, someone who had lured her here for a reason. Was there still a white slave-trade in operation? she wondered.

She rang down to the reception, and asked tetchily whether she had been given the correct room number.

'There are no clothes here,' she said coolly, 'only one ice bucket with champagne in it.'

'There's no mistake, Miss Stanley,' the girl's voice came down the line. 'I'm sure your friend will be with you shortly.'

Well, she thought, replacing the receiver, unless her '*friend*' showed up within the next half an hour she would come to find an empty room.

The situation was ludicrous. All that tension, and here she was, facing one ice bucket with some champagne in it, two prints on the walls and a large double bed with a quilted bedspread.

She paced the room, staring out of the window until the view became too monotonous to continue watching, looking at her watch and at the door, and was about to leave when she heard the porter turning the key in the lock.

At long last.

She stood up, ready to inform Nicole that her pressing appointments would leave her very little time here, when her eyes widened first in surprise, then in horror.

No Nicole. No female, in fact. Just Piers, entering the room with the same easy stride that she remembered so clearly, dressed casually in a pair of beige trousers and a short-sleeved shirt.

'What are you doing here?' Alyssia heard herself whisper, wishing that there were a white slave-trade in operation, because that would have been infinitely preferable to being confronted by him.

Her fingers were gripping her dress, and she knew that she was trembling.

Piers was quick to conceal his surprise. Or was it dismay? she thought acidly.

'I might well ask you the same question,' he said coolly, not moving further into the room.

Alyssia went across to the sofa, still badly shaken,

and sat down. Sitting down was at least one way of controlling the wobbly feeling in her legs.

She didn't look at him. She didn't want to. She just wanted some huge natural catastrophe to sweep through the bedroom and miraculously carry her two hundred thousand miles away.

He went across to the bed and sat on it, staring at her broodingly from under the thick dark lashes.

'I came here to see *your girlfriend*,' she said in an unnaturally high voice. 'If I had thought that I'd bump into you, believe me, I would never have agreed.'

She took in the lean, hard, semi-reclining figure and felt all those humiliating feelings of need surge through her.

It made her more angry with herself than with him.

'Funny, I came here to see her as well.'

'Oh, yes?' Alyssia controlled her features into a frozen expression. 'Although I shouldn't be surprised, should I?'

A rush of violent jealousy swept through her, but she was absolutely determined not to let it show.

Was that what Nicole wanted? she thought bitterly. To tell her that she and Piers were now a going concern? To gloat?

She could see that her remark had hit home. He hadn't been hurt by it, probably not even insulted, but it had made him angry. She could see it in the black expression that crossed his face and the tightened lips.

He walked across to the window, leaning back against it, surveying her with a mixture of contempt and distaste.

'That's a particularly nasty thing to say, but maybe I should have expected it of you.'

His words were like drops of ice, and every one hurt her more than she could have believed possible.

'Meaning?'

'Meaning that I should have trusted my first impressions of you.'

'You should have,' Alyssia agreed woodenly.

How dared he act as though she were the guilty party? As though she should be the one making apologies for her behaviour? 'Although I can't quite understand the little show of self-righteousness. I know all about you and Nicole.'

'Do you, now? And what exactly do you know, or should I even bother to ask? I can imagine just what pictures that sordid mind of yours has concocted.'

'How dare you?' Her face had turned white.

'Still getting angry when someone throws some truth in your face?' he jeered.

He looked away and began twiddling with the curtain cord. Alyssia wished that it would somehow whip around his neck and strangle him on the spot.

'You call that truth?' she spat out, trying to control her rage and failing. 'You wouldn't know how to tell the truth if your life depended on it.'

Any minute now, she thought, she would do the unthinkable and burst into tears. She could feel them welling up behind her eyes, and she blinked rapidly, trying to refocus on how much she hated him instead of how much he was hurting her.

'And what does that mean?'

'What do you think?' she said coldly. 'Pardon me for jumping to erroneous conclusions. After all, here you are in Nicole's hotel bedroom, obviously believing that you weren't going to be finding a third party here as well. I suppose you'll be telling me next that most normal people would immediately asume that you were here to discuss the state of French politics!'

This time he moved across to her, and she flinched back, not caring for the threatening look on his face.

He placed his hands on either side of her, and stared down into her eyes.

'Maybe you're right,' he said with razor-sharp precision, 'maybe I am here to sleep with her. What would you think of that?'

Alyssia's heart was beating ferociously, and there was a throbbing in her temples that was making her feel quite dizzy. Or maybe it was just his proximity having that effect on her.

'Are you?' she asked, desperate to find out. What else, she thought, tormented, would he be doing here?

'Why are you so keen to find out?'

'I'm not,' Alyssia lied quickly. 'I just think that it's disgusting for you to be having an affair with a married woman, that's all.'

For a moment she thought that he was going to hit her, but she continued looking at him mutinously, not caring what he did.

He didn't hit her. He stood up abruptly and walked across to the window, staring outside at the same nondescript view that she herself had spent over fifteen minues staring at earlier on.

Right now, she thought; I could leave right now. There's no bolt on the door. I could walk right out of here and right out of this situation. But she didn't. She was glued to the chair, fascinated by that sharp profile staring down into the street below.

He still hadn't said anything to her bald accusation, and suddenly she needed his reply more than she would have thought possible.

'Are you afraid to say something?' she pursued recklessly, her blonde hair swinging across her shoulders as she raised her face to stare up at him.

'There's nothing in this world that I'm afraid of,' he said smoothly, 'least of all anything I might have to say to you.'

Looking at him now, she knew with certainty that he was telling the truth. There was nothing he was afraid of.

Including, she thought bitterly, playing with her life, throwing it all out of focus and then leaving her.

'But I have no intention of telling you what you want to know.' He looked at her long and hard, then continued softly. 'Or of substantiating all those speculations about me. It's none of your business.'

The silence stretched between them like a length of tightly pulled elastic, and in the silence Alyssia could feel the hammering of her heart like a physical pain.

The sudden shriek of the telephone made her jump.

Who could be phoning here? Then she thought, Nicole. Who else?

She watched him as he snatched the receiver and barked down the end of it, but she hadn't a clue as to the nature of the conversation, since she was privy to only one side, and that was in French.

But there was no doubt that it was the other woman on the line. After the initial impatience in his voice he sounded gentler, less forbidding.

Damn her, she thought. What did she have that gave her such power over him?

When he replaced the receiver she turned to him, her fists clenched at her sides, and said frigidly, 'Nicole, was it? Things not gone quite according to plan?'

'Not quite,' he said, sinking on to the sofa and casually crossing one leg, raking his fingers through his hair.

'And what was the plan? No,' she added fiercely,

'don't answer that one. Why break the habit of a lifetime?'

Their eyes locked together and she was surprised to see that there was no anger in his expression. If anything, he looked unsure.

Or maybe just disappointed, she thought, correcting the impression.

But his expression left her feeling uncertain all of a sudden. She glanced hesitantly at the door.

There was no point in remaining here, that was for sure.

How could she feel her whole body yearning for him, when logic and reason told her that it shouldn't be?

It wasn't fair! Fair was being able to control how she felt. Fair was definitely not being at the beck and call of her wayward emotions.

There was only one way to remedy the situation.

She stood up and grabbed her bag from the floor, taking care to school her expression into a mask of indifference.

'Anyway,' she said, speaking into the silence, and aware that her voice sounded disastrously unsteady, 'there's no point remaining here, is there?' She began walking towards the door. 'I have things to do, and I'm sure you have as well.'

She didn't hear him come up from behind at all.

He moved like a shadow, and the first thing she knew of his presence behind her was when he got hold of her arm, forcing her to turn around.

'Wait,' he said in a low voice, and Alyssia stopped dead in her tracks. She had no choice. The mere touch of his fingers on her arm was making her head spin.

'You seem to make a habit of this,' she muttered as confusion propelled her into action. She tried tugging at his arm, but this time he didn't release her even slightly.

'Only with you.'

'If you don't let me go, *this instant*,' she said, raising her voice a pitch higher, 'I'm going to scream the place down. I'll have everybody in the hotel racing into this room to find out exactly what's happening.'

'Well, then,' he murmured, 'there's one way of stopping that, isn't there?'

CHAPTER TEN

ALYSSIA saw the burning intensity in his grey eyes, and then Piers bent his head towards hers, kissing her fiercely.

She gave a little whimper of denial, her flat fists pushing against his chest, but he had moved his hand behind her head and was pressing her against him, forcing her lips apart so that he could savage her mouth with his tongue.

Passion whipped through her, a raging fire that started in the pit of her stomach and swept through every other part of her body.

All she wanted to do was yield to it, because it was what she had wanted for the whole time she had been with him.

'No!' she cried, as much to herself as to him.

'No? Why?' he muttered hoarsely.

'We have to talk about this rationally,' she tried, her body quivering from his onslaught.

'There's nothing rational about what I feel!'

Nor I, she thought in panic. Reason had grown wings and flown out of the window, but she knew that she had to recapture it or else give in to him, and live to regret her weakness.

He grasped her long hair, so that strands of silk fell through his fingers, and tugged her head back gently, kissing her on her neck, muttering things that she could barely hear, far less understand.

If I don't take control of things at once, she thought,

I never will. I'll spend the rest of my life knowing that I was willingly used by a man who didn't love me.

She forced her body to stiffen, to fight off his attack, but it was mental agony.

'You can't do this to me,' she said unsteadily.

'I'm not doing anything to you,' he breathed into her ear, 'we're doing it to each other.'

'And what if I had never shown up here? Would you and Nicole be doing this to each other right now?'

He pulled back from her and stared into her eyes. 'You want to talk?' he asked her roughly. 'Then we'll talk.'

'Not here.'

'Afraid?' he mocked.

He had still not released her hair, and he guided her firmly towards the sofa and sat her down, sitting beside her but very close, as though warning her that she couldn't escape if that was what she intended.

'Of what?'

'Of me.' He looked around the room. 'Of that bed sitting over there. Of the fact that, however hard you try to adopt that indifferent expression, underneath you want me every bit as much as I want you.'

'Want, want, want,' Alyssia repeated bitterly; 'is that the only word in your vocabulary?'

The grey eyes roamed over her face, and she felt as though she was being devoured by some huge magnetic force.

'No,' he said softly, 'it's not the only word in my vocabulary. I need you. I didn't realise how much until you ran away.'

'I didn't run away,' she muttered in a shaky voice. He needed her! It should have sent her spirits soaring, but it didn't, because wasn't need just another aspect of lust?

He didn't need her because of her wonderful personality. He needed her because of her wonderful body.

Men had always talked to her about need, and about love as well, but in a voice that didn't differentiate the two. She had always laughed, enjoyed the flattery, never expecting love from any of them because she had not loved any of them herself, but this time was different.

She loved Piers, and it just wasn't good enough to be told that he needed her or that he wanted her.

'You did run away,' he muttered, 'but that didn't stop me needing you.'

'People don't need each other,' she said in a low voice, 'they need food, water, air.'

'You're playing with words.'

And you, she thought, are playing with me, just as you played with me in France. *And where does Nicole fit into all this?*

She shook her head free of his grip, and sat further away on the sofa, looking at him with detachment.

He really was magnificent. It amazed her that she had not thought that the minute she had met him, or maybe she had but had simply denied it to herself.

'Why did you come here to meet Nicole?' she asked. 'In a hotel bedroom, of all places. We have to talk about her.'

'Is that what's bothering you? Are you jealous because you think that I came here to sleep with her?' He waved aside her automatic protest, and then sighed heavily. 'You're right, we have to talk about Nicole, and a lot more besides.'

She waited, holding her breath, wondering whether he would really answer all the questions that had been buzzing around in her head ever since she had first met him, or whether he would skirt around the subject and depend instead on the overwhelming attraction she felt for him to talk her back into bed.

'I'm waiting,' Alyssia said tensely.

He reached out and brushed a strand of hair away from her face, and she felt her skin tingle where it had been touched.

They were talking rationally now, as adults, just as she had asked, but underneath the façade of civilised behaviour her heart was still doing funny things, and the electricity between them was as powerful as if they had been making love.

'Why did you agree to meet her in the first place?' She had to know. It was the question that had been tormenting her from the very moment she had seen him enter the room. 'What does she mean to you? I have to know.'

He looked away and a dark flush spread through his face, making him look suddenly very vulnerable.

'What does Nicole mean to me?' He rubbed his eyes. 'It's not what you think.'

'Explain it to me, and let me decide.'

'All right.' He stood up and began prowling around the room, touching objects, focusing his attention on anything but her.

'I met Nicole years ago—seven years ago, to be exact.' He sat back down next to her, but he still didn't look at her, and she had a sinking feeling that he really was going to tell her the truth about Nicole, but it would not be to her liking.

If he was not in love with the other woman, as he seemed to have implied, then why the fuss? Why the desire to keep it to himself? No, there was much more to it than that, and it was the much more that was now making her heart constrict.

She looked away, staring fixedly at the dressing-table just behind him.

'I had just finished my university course, and my first job was in the south of France, very close to that little village where your house is.'

'Hence the willingness to put yourself out and do that favour for my father,' she said dully. 'You were only doing it for yourself, using it as an excuse to go back in time and relive old memories.'

'Subconsciously, yes, I suppose so.'

'You met Nicole there, didn't you? That's where your grand affair began.' God, it hurt to say those words. She knew what would come now, and automatically switched off.

'I know that's what you imagine, and I guess I've let you believe that because I had become so accustomed to my privacy that I didn't care for your intrusion into it, but you're wrong. I am not in love with Nicole and I never have been.'

Alyssia raised startled eyes to his. 'What do you mean?'

'I mean. . .' He paused, and she sensed that he was finding it difficult to express his thoughts. 'I mean that we go back a long way, and yes, there's a very special relationship between us, but that's because. . .' another pause, and he raked his fingers through his hair in a helpless, frustrated gesture '. . .it was her sister I fell in love with all those years ago.'

'Her sister? But——'

'But you haven't met any sister?'

She nodded mutely.

'That's because she died in a car accident five years ago.'

There was a long silence while Alyssia assimilated

this information. It was so totally unexpected that she could hardly comprehend it.

'I'm so sorry,' she said at last.

He stood up abruptly and resumed his restless pacing of the room, like a caged animal that had suddenly found the confines of its cage far too small for comfort.

She wanted desperately to reach out to him, but she knew that she had to wait for him to make the first move. After all, would he be telling her all this now if this meeting had not been arranged? It was a question that seemed of crucial importance.

'And if Nicole hadn't arranged this meeeting?' she asked.

'I was returning to London anyway. Of course I would have contacted you. We slept together!'

'Of course,' Alyssia mocked, 'we did.'

'Did you think that I would make love to you for a few days and then let you walk out of my life without trying to get in touch?'

'And would you have told me about her sister?'

There was a long silence. She licked her lips nervously, and realised that she was sitting on the edge of the sofa, staring at him as though her life depended on it. Being a little fool again. He hadn't said anything that had given her any indication that he actually cared for her.

She forced herself to relax.

'I would have told you,' he muttered, looking away.

'Why not sooner?'

'I wasn't ready. I wasn't ready to share my life with anyone. My bed, fine, but my life. . .that was something that had always been untouchable, and, as far as I was concerned, always would be. I loved Jeanne and I was devastated when she died. She was so young, so full of life. I shut myself off from the female race and channelled all my energy into my work. I was absolutely determined not to expose myself to the sort of pain that love can bring.'

He looked at her steadily, and her heart flipped over.

'Go on,' she whispered.

'And then,' he said, 'you came along. You did something to me. For starters, I wanted you the way I never thought I would ever want anyone again.'

He came towards her, covering her mouth possessively with his own, and Alyssia felt her senses begin to swim. This time she made no effort to fight him. The desire burning inside her was too strong, and she returned his kiss, hearing him moan at her response. Her fingers wound into his hair, guiding his head to her neck.

He pushed her back against the sofa, covering her body with his, devouring her with his mouth.

'I want you, Alyssia. I thought I would go mad when you left France and I returned to an empty house.'

But what about love? she wanted to cry out.

What will happen when this want dies? She saw her future flash in front of her like a dying man's, every day longer and emptier than the one before.

As though reading her mind, he released her and looked down at her face, the intensity of his stare making her flush.

'You came,' he said, 'with your argumentative aggravating, adorable ways, and I could feel my invulnerability slipping away.'

Alyssia hardly dared look at him.

'You don't just want my body?' she ventured timidly. 'Am I simply a substitute for Jeanne?'

'No,' he said softly. 'I don't, and you're not. Don't you think that I could find other, just as exceptional bodies somewhere else?'

He sighed heavily. He sounded like a man who had tried every permutation to unlock a safe, and finally had to admit that he was baffled.

'The truth is that I fought what I felt for you for as long as I could, and even after we made love I told myself that I wanted you, desperately, but that you meant nothing more to me than an object of desire.'

Alyssia looked at his face and felt a smile twitch the corners of her mouth. She raised her hand and stroked his face, and he caught it with his own, turning it over so that it was palm up, and kissing it.

'You're an enchanting woman,' he muttered, 'I tried to keep my distance from you, but you bewitched me. That's why I slept with you. I couldn't understand it, couldn't understand how I could have found myself so violently drawn to someone so. . .'

'Childish?'

'That was part of your appeal. Only I realised it too late.'

Before she was aware of what he was doing, he had lifted her up and was carrying her to the bed, where he deposited her gently, like some priceless, fragile object.

She looked at him with drowsy, yearning eyes. When his mouth moved to caress her breasts she moaned with pleasure, guiding his head towards her stomach.

Her breath was coming in short bursts. The brief pause while he slipped off his clothing was like agony; then he was next to her, hard and demanding.

He parted her thighs, caressing them with his fingers, exploring every inch of her until her body was throbbing with need.

He moved up to kiss her while his hand continued to stroke her aching body, then, when neither of them could bear it any longer, he thrust into her, and she arched back, drowning under wave after wave of mounting pleasure.

His mouth was savage on hers, his hands cupping her breast, rolling the nipple between his fingers.

Alyssia closed her eyes and flung back her head, savouring his passion.

'I've thought of nothing but you ever since you left,' he murmured against her. 'Why do you think Nicole arranged this meeting? I was driving her crazy with my impotent rage at your absence.'

Her hand gripped the small of his back until they lay spent next to each other on the bed.

Damned tears, she thought angrily, but she could not stop them. They trickled down her cheeks, and Piers looked at her, alarmed.

'What's the matter?' he asked urgently. 'Why the tears? Have I hurt you somehow?'

Alyssia shook her head.

He propped himself on his elbow and stared at her. 'Then what? What have I done? Don't you know that I would never hurt you?'

'Never?' she enquired sadly.

'Never. As long as I live.'

Her heart gave a sudden leap. She looked at him and he looked away. 'Don't you mean, as long as we're together?' In other words, she wanted to add, until you've had your fill of me?

'That's what I mean,' he said gruffly.

'I don't understand.' She thought she did, but she couldn't trust herself to interpret correctly what he was telling her. She couldn't allow herself that brief moment of hope, only to find herself right back where she had started.

'I love you, Alyssia. I tried damned hard to hide it from myself, but I can't hide it any longer.'

She smiled, a glittering smile of pure happiness.

'I love you too,' she said.

He tilted her chin towards him. 'I guessed as much. My darling, that was one of the things I found so bloody irresistible about you. But it turns me on just to hear you say it.'

'And Jeanne?'

'I'll always have memories of her, of course, but she's in the past now. You're the one who fills my head and my heart. Nicole saw it long before I did. Do you know that it took all my self-control not to throttle that dim-witted boy?'

'André?' She giggled.

'Um. Now I know there's only one thing for me to do.'

'What's that?'

'Marry you, of course.'

This, she thought, nestling against him, was heaven. Who could ever have told her that love could be this good?

The sun was shining this time, but Alyssia would have remembered that little house anywhere. She twined her fingers through Piers's and tugged him towards the door.

'This is ridiculous,' he said under his breath, but his smile was indulgent. 'I'll put it down to pre-wedding madness, and hope that it doesn't strike again.'

Alyssia grinned and knocked on the door. For the past five days now she had been living somewhere on cloud nine, and had decided that she might just as well set up home there, as it was such a wonderful place to be.

The door was opened almost immediately, even though this time no appointment had been made.

'I don't know if you remember me,' Alyssia began.

'Of course I do.' Claire grinned, the same infectious grin that Alyssia remembered, and ushered them in.

'This,' she said, making her introductions, 'is Piers. A sceptic.'

He grinned reluctantly, his powerful body dominating the tiny hallway. 'She virtually kidnapped me to bring me here,' he said.

Claire looked at him shrewdly. 'Virgo?' she asked.

He looked at her, startled. 'How did you know?'

'An informed guess.'

'We're to be married in two weeks' time,' Alyssia informed her, settling into one of the chairs with Piers's arm protectively resting behind her shoulders.

'If you had stayed to hear what I had left to say,' Claire said, smiling, 'instead of rushing out in the rain, I would have told you that, at the end of your dark tunnel, you would eventually reach the light.'

'And you could see all that?' Piers drawled.

'You really are a sceptic! Do sceptics drink cups of tea?'

She prepared some tea for them, chatting about generalities, asking them what had brought them back to France.

'Some work,' Piers said, 'on a certain house, which wasn't finished quite according to schedule because of a certain lady who turned my world upside-down.'

'So,' Alyssia joined in, 'we thought we'd drop by and let you know that everything worked out in the end. And to tell you that you were amazingly accurate in certain areas. But why didn't you tell me that things would work out?'

'Because you didn't want to stay to find out,' Claire said simply.

'I hate to interject a note of boring realism here,' Piers said, 'but isn't it easy to say that in retrospect?'

They had finished their cups of tea and he stood to leave.

Claire laughed. 'So it is,' she agreed, 'but before you go I want to give you something.'

She hurried off and returned a few minutes later with a tiny white gown.

'It's beautiful,' Alyssia said, holding it up, noticing the delicate embroidery on it. 'But what is it for?'

Claire opened the front door, letting in a cool summery breeze. 'It's for the baby that you will have in ten months' time.'

They could still hear her tinkling laughter as the door closed behind them. Piers pulled her close to him.

'Well,' he said, 'we'll just have to get to the house and start proving that this particular astrologer has her finger on the button, won't we?'

'Whatever do you mean?' Alyssia asked with mock innocence.

She laughed as his warm mouth against hers told her exactly what he had in mind!

STARGAZING

YOUR STAR SIGN: **VIRGO (August 24th–September 23rd)**

VIRGO is the second of the Earth signs and is ruled by the planet Mercury, which makes you cautious, restrained and practical. You crave order and control in your life and so have a tendency to fuss and criticise, although you find as many faults in yourself as in others. You love children, but you must remember that you can't expect them to be as tidy as you like to be! You are an excellent communicator and have uncanny intuitive powers but your jealousy and possessiveness will often threaten good friendships. Yet you are generous and warm-hearted—despite all the moaning!

Your characteristics in love: Virgoans can seem shy and are often cautious about making the first move in a relationship but, motivated by your desire to love and be loved, you really work hard to keep the magic alive. You expect perfection and tend to nag your partner but you set yourself high standards too and, because you hate deceit in others, you yourself will always be loyal and trustworthy. You believe in the importance of personal privacy and you are happiest if you can keep some degree of space and independence. As a lover, you value touch and togetherness, and sensuality rather than sexuality—but watch out: Virgoan women can suddenly find themselves passionately attracted to the most unlikely men!

Signs which are compatible with you: You can find harmony with **Taurus**, **Capricorn**, **Cancer** and **Scorpio**—but expect fireworks with **Pisces**, **Sagittarius** and **Gemini**! Partners born under other signs can be compatible, depending on which planets reside in their Houses of Personality and Romance.

What is your star-career? Whatever your chosen career, Virgoans are responsible, efficient, clear-thinking and often workaholics. You enjoy turning chaos into order and so, for an opportunity to display your organising skills and fine discrimination, careers in publishing, administration, education, health, catering, secretarial work or banking should appeal to you.

Your colours and birthstones: Virgoans, with their natural fastidiousness, love the purity of stark white.

One of your birthstones, the dark blue sapphire, is said to act directly on the intellect and is also thought to be subconsciously chosen by all those who wish to suppress their emotions, as Virgoans try to do. Another ideal present for a Virgoan woman is sardonyx, from which cameo brooches are made. This stone is said to inspire romance in those who wear it.

VIRGO ASTRO-FACTFILE

Day of the week: Wednesday
Countries: Austria, Norway
Flowers: Small flowers, hyacinth
Food: Carrots, celery, apples and raspberries. Virgoans are very health-conscious and prefer to bake, steam or grill rather than fry, and like to use low fat and whole foods in their cooking. But as a treat, you love a fresh cream cake!
Health: As an earth sign you know the importance of exercise and good diet but you can be rather a hypochondriac, so try not to get obsessive about your health!

You share your star sign with these famous names:

Lauren Bacall
Sophia Loren
Twiggy
Shirley Conran
Raquel Welch

Sean Connery
Richard Gere
Roald Dahl
Frederick Forsyth
Michael Jackson

Next Month's Romances

Each month you can choose from a world of variety in romance with Mills & Boon. Below are the new titles to look out for next month, why not ask either Mills & Boon Reader Service or your Newsagent to reserve you a copy of the titles you want to buy — just tick the titles you would like to order and either post to Reader Service or take it to any Newsagent and ask them to order your books.

Please save me the following titles:		Please tick	√
A HONEYED SEDUCTION	Diana Hamilton		
PASSIONATE POSSESSION	Penny Jordan		
MOTHER OF THE BRIDE	Carole Mortimer		
DARK ILLUSION	Patricia Wilson		
FATE OF HAPPINESS	Emma Richmond		
THE ALPHA MAN	Kay Thorpe		
HUNGARIAN RHAPSODY (This book is free with THE ALPHA MAN)	Jessica Steele		
NOTHING LESS THAN LOVE	Vanessa Grant		
LOVE'S VENDETTA	Stephanie Howard		
CALL UP THE WIND	Anne McAllister		
TOUCH OF FIRE	Joanna Neil		
TOMORROW'S HARVEST	Alison York		
THE STOLEN HEART	Amanda Browning		
NO MISTAKING LOVE	Jessica Hart		
THE BEGINNING OF THE AFFAIR	Marjorie Lewty		
CAUSE FOR LOVE	Kerry Allyne		
RAPTURE IN THE SANDS	Sandra Marton		

If you would like to order these books from Mills & Boon Reader Service please send £1.70 per title to: Mills & Boon Reader Service, P.O. Box 236, Croydon, Surrey, CR9 3RU and quote your Subscriber No:...(If applicable) and complete the name and address details below. Alternatively, these books are available from many local Newsagents including W.H.Smith, J.Menzies, Martins and other paperback stockists from 11th September 1992.

Name:...

Address:..

....Post Code:......................

To Retailer: If you would like to stock M&B books please contact your regular book/magazine wholesaler for details.